LONG ROAD HOME

Chris Orr

Cover photo by Lisa O'Donnell

*To my dear wife, Hilda, for all her love and encouragement
to me in getting this book written and published.*

Chapter 1

Ireland 1842

Thomas lay back in the long grass and gazed out at his favourite view. From the top of the cliff he could see for miles, and today there was even a glimpse of Scotland in the distance. Kinnego Bay was sheltered from the westerly winds with a natural curve, making it one of the best beaches in Ireland, hidden away from most of the world.

Mary was sitting on his right, deep in thought, as she chewed a sliver of long grass. She was twenty and incredibly beautiful. She had the most startling blue eyes and long, silky black hair; an unusual combination, since most Donegal girls had either auburn or red hair. Mary was like a sister to Thomas as they had spent so much time in each other's homes.

He had just recently noticed just how lovely she was, and sometimes wondered if one day they might marry - but no, they were just friends - soul mates, in fact. They could talk about anything and everything. Their houses were only a few furlongs apart, with the closest neighbour's house nearly a day's walk away, but often there was very little local activity for them to talk about, so they were content to just sit silently enjoying each other's company. Today was a perfect day for that. Spring had very definitely arrived and with it enough sunshine to sit without winter coats.

The Donegal folk were poor, and the locals survived on small farms, with the man of the house having to travel long distances to find work. Thomas's father, Patrick, lived in a rented cottage owned by the English landlord who lived in a large estate near Moville on the banks of the river Foyle, eight miles east of Kinnego Bay. Apart from keeping a few chickens, Patrick made his living from the sea in his small curragh.

The curragh, a flimsy wooden framed boat covered in a pitch canvas, and was light enough for one man to carry it down the beach. Even though it was light, however, it was very sea worthy, and could stand any strong wave without being damaged. Patrick shared the boat with his neighbour and lifelong friend, Fergal, Mary's father.

Patrick's parents had both died when Patrick was in his twenties and, as an only child, he had struggled to keep the farm going. Eventually, he had to sell it and move to a rented cottage owned by the English landlord from Moville. He was very clever, and often invented new ways of doing things, but sadly never had the money to pursue his dream of becoming an engineer. He now hoped that one day Thomas would follow in his footsteps.

Patrick's friend, Fergal, owned his own cottage with sixty acres of decent agricultural land. He was better off than most in Donegal at that time, as he had a few cows and sheep and grew a few acres of potatoes which he sold in nearby towns in the summer. Like Patrick, fishing was his real work, and he regarded the rest as just a distraction until he could get into his boat and sail away for the day.

'What are you thinking about Mary,' Thomas asked, contentedly. She turned and looked at her best friend. How she loved him! He was kind, smart, funny but quite serious at times as well. She never wanted things to change and the thought of them ever being parted filled her with dread.

'I love this place Thomas.' She paused, smiling and rubbing the grass between her hands, 'but I'm afraid that it will all end one day.'

Thomas sat up and took her arm in his gentle hands. 'Don't say that

Mary! Why on earth would this end?'

'Well, it was just because of a bad dream I had the other night. I don't really remember all of it, but it was very scary. I was convinced at that moment that bad things were about to change our lives forever.' She looked troubled for a second.

'Don't talk like that Mary. Sure, what could ever go wrong in Donegal? I mean, nothing ever happens here at all, let alone something bad!'

'I know Thomas,' she laughed getting up, 'let's go for a run in the grass. I'll beat ye again.'

With that the two were off running through the long grass back towards the top of the hill.

Little did Thomas know that Mary's dream was a dark premonition of things to come, but right now, running in the grass with his best friend was the best thing in his life. She beat him to the top and laughed. 'I thought you men could beat us women at anything.'

'I would like to see you stack the turf then, woman, on a cold September day!'

'No bother to me, lad. Look at my muscles,' she retorted playfully, pulling up the sleeve of her dress. Thomas grabbed he arm gently.

'Ah sure there's nothing there at all Mary.' With that he laughed and jumped over the ditch.

'Beat ye home,' she heard, as he disappeared down the track.

When Mary arrived at her house Thomas was sitting on a stone by the front door pretending to be asleep in the sun. Mary's mother, Rose, came out the door as she arrived panting.

'Where have you been, girl?' she scolded.

'My fault Rose,' said Thomas jumping up. 'I took her to the bay.' Rose looked at Thomas and realised he was growing into a fine man like his father. One day he might make a good husband for her Mary.

'There's too much for you to do, girl, without going on a daydream at the bay and, Thomas, have you no work to do at your own house on this spring day?' she chided lightly.

'Ay, Mrs Rose. I'd better get home as my da's away fishing with Fergal. See you tomorrow Mary.'

'He's a good man, Ma. I'd be lost without him,' Mary sighed.

'I know, Mary. That's what I'm worried about.'

Thomas ran over the hill that led to his cottage, and was surprised to see his father coming towards him with a large fishing net on his back.

'I thought you were away out in the boat, Da?' said Thomas.

'I had to come back for our spare net as we found a big hole in our main one,' Patrick grumbled, 'but we'll be off now. Your mother was looking for you to take the horse over to the blacksmith to get shod.'

Thomas tried to hide his excitement as he loved doing anything with the horse, and today he was being trusted to ride four miles. 'Don't even think of going faster than a walk,' his father warned him as he passed. 'I'll know if you do.'

'I won't, Da. I'll go as slow as slow can be,' he reassured him, smiling.

Patrick stopped and studied his son, who was suddenly becoming a man. He felt sad that he was having to live in a time where there was very little future for him. Thomas noticed his father looking at him, but his thoughts were elsewhere. He suddenly remembered that tomorrow was his eighteenth birthday.

'Do you know what day it is tomorrow, Da?'

'Tuesday, Thomas. It's Tuesday. Why?' replied Patrick quietly.

'It's not only Tuesday; it's my birthday.' He paused and took a deep breath. 'You always told me that I could go fishing with you when I turned eighteen.'

Patrick stopped and looked down. His heart sank, but he tried not to show it. This was the last thing he wanted for his son, but he had made a promise to him when he was six years old and his son had reminded him every year on his birthday ever since. He saw the excitement in Thomas's eyes and knew there was no way out. He turned back with his heavy load and heavy heart as he walked slowly up the track to the bay.

'Make sure your mother has warm clothes for you for the morning.' Thomas ran like the wind back to his house, hardly able to contain his excitement.

His mother was waiting for him at the stone wall that surrounded the small cottage. The white cottage needed repair, and the thatch roof was starting to leak and fall apart. There was no need for Thomas to say anything as he could see he was in trouble for sneaking off with Mary. She watched him silently as he slipped around the back of the house to the small stable shared by all the farm animals. Anxiously she bit her lip, knowing that it would be a waste of time to try and stop her son following his father into fishing, and yet she longed for something else to come along.

Thomas put a halter on the large brown hunter and led him out of the stable to saddle him up. The horse was old and very quiet, and Patrick only used him to help the other small farmers who needed their fields ploughed. He had bought the horse many years before at a fair when he had too much to drink and then discovered that no neighbours had enough land to warrant keeping a horse and plough. He was now stuck with it and could barely afford to feed it in the winter. It had caused many a row between him and his wife.

As Thomas threw the saddle over the horse's back, his mother poked her head around the shed door. 'Make sure that girth's tight enough, son,' she warned. 'You don't want the saddle sliding off on you down the road.' Thomas tightened the last strap and came around to his mother.

'It's ok, Ma. This old thing can only walk. Don't worry. I'll be careful.'

'Ye better, son. See if the blacksmith might want to buy the old nag.' She patted the horse, laughing, 'I'll get rid of the old thing yet.'

'Ma,' Thomas ventured quietly as he turned the horse for the gate, 'I'm going fishing with Da in the morning.'

'What!' 'Fishing?'

'I'm eighteen tomorrow and Da promised me that would be the day I could go with him.'

She dropped her head and Thomas could see she was upset.

'Just for a day, Ma. I've dreamed of it all my life. Just for one day.'

Bridget turned and walked back to the cottage. He would have followed her into the house only the horse was now impatient to get on the road, and he thought it best to move on.

It was getting dark by the time Thomas returned, and he could see his mother had already lit the oil lamp in the kitchen. His father was arriving at the same time from the opposite direction with a couple of sea trout hanging on a stick over his shoulder.

'Well, lad?' he asked as he grabbed the halter and let his son dismount.

'It only needed one shoe, Da, as the man said the others would do a few months yet.'

'How much did he charge?'

'Nothing,' replied Thomas, handing the horse over to his dad. 'He said he owed you a favour for the fish.' Patrick looked down at the ground and said nothing.

'Right, son. Better get in to your ma and get some sleep. We're leaving at dawn tomorrow.'

Thomas slumped into the kitchen chair and his mother handed him a plate of stew. He supped it slowly, blissfully unaware of the events which were about to unfold.

Chapter 2

The next morning was even more like summer than the day before. Thomas was up and dressed and had even eaten his porridge before his father appeared.

'Ma isn't too happy at you coming with me to fish today, Thomas.' Patrick started, as he poured himself some tea. Thomas's heart sank at the thought of his dad changing his mind. He continued, 'I told her we would only go a short run today and be back by mid-afternoon, so get your coat, lad. It can get cold out there, even when it's warm on the shore.'

'Is Fergal coming, Da?' Thomas asked, as they made their way down the steep path to Kinnego Bay.

'Of course, son. I would never go fishing without Fergal and, after all, he owns the boat!'

Thomas took a deep breath of the crisp morning sea air and he felt that he was going to burst with excitement. He could see Fergal was already working at the up-turned curragh on the shore.

'I put an extra patch and tar on the bow section,' Fergal said as they approached the boat. 'I noticed a tiny drop of water coming in yesterday, but it should be fine now.'

Patrick and Fergal held each end of the boat and turned it over. 'Looks grand, Fergal.' Patrick rubbed the new joint. 'I'm surprised it's set already. Grab the bag Thomas and let's be off.'

The two men carried the curragh to the water while Thomas lifted the bag and the two oars. The tide was well out, which meant they could launch the boat from the rocks instead of getting wet wading into the sea.

'In ye get, Thomas,' said Fergal taking the oars from him, 'and put the bag under the back seat.'

The two men climbed in and sat beside each other while Thomas sat at the back. Seagulls were making a terrible noise as they pushed off.

'That's not a good sign,' said Fergal, starting to pull hard on the oars. Patrick turned and looked out to sea. 'Looks all right to me, Fergal. Not a cloud in the sky.'

Within an hour, they were nearly two miles out from land and it was time to drop the nets. When the men stood up the boat rolled precariously, and Thomas grabbed the seat. 'It's all right, son.' It'll roll right onto its side without going over. Just hang on tight.' Thomas wasn't convinced, though, and wondered if this really was a good idea after all. The men threw the nets in and started chatting about the price of cattle, the crops and other matters.

After four hours Thomas noticed the sea was beginning to get waves. The curragh began to move up and down as the gentle rollers got bigger. He felt a breeze for the first time and pulled his coat up as the air was getting cooler. Fergal asked for the bag under Thomas' seat and produced some sandwiches that Rose had made that morning. Thomas thought that the sandwich never tasted as good as it did right now. He was very hungry.

'The sea air makes you eat like a horse, Thomas,' his dad laughed, as he watched his son devour the whole sandwich in three bites. 'Maybe that's what we should do with our old mare.'

They all laughed as Fergal looked down at the nets.

'I think we will pull all in now, Patrick. I think I saw a big salmon.' They dropped their sandwich and grabbed the net line and started pulling. Sure enough, as the nets appeared they were full of fish, including two eight-pound salmon.

'Look at this, Fergal!' shouted Patrick excitedly. 'There's enough here to pay the rent for a month!' The boat was practically on its side now and Thomas was sure it was going to capsize. He moved to the other side and leaned out to try and balance it. Within a few minutes the floor of the boat was filled with fish and the men returned to their seat.

Just then, Thomas looked out past them and realised there was a thick black cloud blowing towards them from the west. 'The sea's gettin' a bit rough, Da,' Thomas said, slightly troubled.

'I did notice that,' Fergal replied, trying not to show his concern.

'Look at that, Da.' Thomas pointed behind them.

The two men turned together and stared at the dark menacing clouds. They turned back to Thomas with concerned faces. 'The seagulls knew something was up, Fergal.'

Patrick grabbed the oar and started to turn the boat. 'It's going to be a tight run home.'

'Hold on, son.' Thomas had never seen his father afraid before, and he knew that something was wrong.

'It's all my fault. I should never have told them about my birthday,' he thought.

The wind and the sea were now in their backs and the curragh was speeding through the sea like it had a sail. The waves were now six feet high, and every time they went down into a trough Thomas lost sight of the land. They were a mile off shore and the boat was surfing on the growing waves. Thomas had never seen two men row as hard before and they both looked exhausted. Every time he looked back, the waves looked bigger. The blue sky was now gone, and the sea was a black as a winter's day. A wave from behind came up suddenly and Thomas got soaked as it broke into the back of the boat. He looked down and could see the boat now had about four inches of water in it. The two men were mustering every ounce of strength as they tried to surf each wave that hit them from behind.

'Hold on tight Thomas,' Fergal shouted above the noise of the storm. Thomas looked at his father. He thought he detected a look of panic, but also of deep sadness.

Suddenly, there was complete darkness.

Thomas felt the ice cold of the spring Atlantic sucking him under. He looked up and realised he was under the sea looking up at light from above. He was choking, but then a great feeling of peace came over him as if he was in a dream. Then the blackness engulfed him once again.

Mary was helping her young sister, Martha, feed the chickens. 'Not like that,' she laughed as the fourteen-year-old threw the whole bucket of grain on the ground. 'That would do a week, Martha, and we don't have a lot left. Take a wee handful and drop a wee bit here and there.'

Martha, who had long red hair and a ruddy complexion, was more like her mother than her sister. There was a six year gap between them, and this, combined with the fact that Martha, who was regarded as being a bit slow, meant that Mary took more of a motherly attitude towards her. She was only now beginning to speak properly, but she loved all animals and would try and pet the chickens, even though they would sometimes react by pecking her on her arms.

It was midday and Mary suddenly felt a cold blast of air come up from the sea. 'That's very strange Martha,' she said, holding her sister's face in her hands, 'on such a warm spring day.' She turned and looked out at the sea and thought about Thomas out fishing with her father, noticing a dark cloud on the horizon out to the west. She wondered where they were fishing today.

Suddenly, a dark feeling came over her and she remembered her dream from two nights ago. She stood upright, letting go of her sister, gazing at the advancing storm clouds. 'Dear God, keep them safe today,' she prayed. 'Please keep them safe.' Her sister looked up at her. 'Who you talking to Mary?' she smiled. 'God, Martha, just God,' she answered softly.

'God?'

'Yes. He's the one who made you so very special.'

'Oh, can I talk to him too then?'

'Sure, you can Martha. Just ask him to take care of Da right now.' Then she stood up.

'Ma. I'm going down to the beach to meet Da and Thomas and make sure they're safe.'

Rose appeared and saw the anxious look in Mary's eyes. She brought Martha into the kitchen and gave her some bread.

'What's wrong Mary?'

'I don't know, Ma. I've a bad feeling. I had a dream the other night that bad things were going to happen, and now I feel they have. She grabbed her shawl from the chair and made for the door. 'I'll be back soon, Ma. Please pray.' With that she ran down the path and headed for the beach.

By the time, Mary got to the top of lane leading down to the strand she was amazed at how bad the storm had got. The six-foot waves were crashing onto the beach and sand was blowing everywhere. She knew that the curragh would never stand a storm like that, so she just presumed that the men had already got back to shore. As she turned the corner she expected to see the curragh sitting in its usual spot high up the beach - but nothing was there.

'Oh, God no!' she said to herself. 'They can't be out in that sea!' She ran to the water's edge and tried to look out to sea. The wind was blowing strong, straight into her face, making her eyes water. All she could see was wave after wave breaking in front of her. The rocks were covered by the incoming tide and a blustering rain was now adding to the storm. She was now in a panic and began to run up and down the strand to see if she could see the boat. She thought if she went to the far end of the beach and climbed up the rocks a bit she might see better out to sea. She ran and tripped on her long skirt and fell face first on the sand.

'Thomas!' she cried, but the noise of the wind drowned her own voice. 'Da!'

She climbed up the small rock and looked out west. Nothing. 'Where could they be?' she thought. If they knew the storm was coming, they might have pulled in to the bay around the headland. She remembered then her father had told her the bay was too dangerous for a boat to land, so they wouldn't have gone there.

Suddenly she thought she saw something in the water. She couldn't see exactly what it was. It might have been her imagination. The light was fading, and it was now difficult to make out anything but a mass of white waves pounding on the shore. She ran back to the west side of the beach and looked again at the area where she thought she saw something. There it was again as a wave now crashed the boat onto the shore. She felt sick in her stomach and thought she was going to faint. It was the curragh - with no one in it!

The next wave pushed the boat further up the shore and Mary grabbed the bow and try to pull it out of the surf. She could see now there were holes in it and all the seats had been broken away from the frame. She fell against the side of the boat and cried and cried.

Mary could hardly walk by the time she reached her home. Rose was standing by the door with a lamp in her hand. 'Where have you been, girl?' she asked crossly. 'I couldn't leave Martha to go and look for you. Where are the men?'

'Oh Ma,' sobbed Mary as she fell into her mother's arms. 'The boat is wrecked and there's no sign of any of them.'.

'It's all right Mary. Maybe they got out before the boat sank. We will find them.'

Thomas tried to open his eyes, but he was face down in the sand. He moved his head to one side, but it ached so badly. He began losing consciousness. A minute later he came around again and tried to take a breath. His lungs hurt terribly when he coughed. He was so cold - ice cold. He moved an arm and tried to brush the sand off his face, but he felt so weak. Just then he heard a voice he thought he recognized.

'He's over here! Over here!' Mary shouted.

The next thing Thomas felt was the warmth of a girl's touch as she tried to turn him over. 'Oh, Thomas, you're alive!' The girl was crying. Thomas couldn't understand why this girl was so upset, and he had no idea who she was or where he was.

Just then four men arrived and lifted Thomas onto an old broken shed door. 'We need to get him home fast. Mary,' said one of the men. 'Go and see if there is any sign of your da and Thomas's da.'

'I don't want to leave Thomas,' she cried.

Every step the men took caused Thomas to wince with the searing pain throughout his entire body. As they reached the path leading to his parent's house, Bridget, who was waiting by the door, came running out to meet them.

'He's alive, Mrs. Sweeney! You need to get him by the fire.' The men put the door down and the strongest one lifted Thomas in his arms and carried him into the house.

'Any sign of Patrick, Charles?' Bridget asked, trembling, as she started to undress Thomas.

'Not yet, Mrs. Sweeney, but if we've found Thomas we may well find your man.' With that he turned away and walked out the door.

'Ye better wait outside for a minute, Mary, till I get Thomas undressed,' said Bridget. Fear was beginning to grip her, but she must look after her son.

Chapter 3

Sir William Campbell marched into the drawing room of his estate house. The maid was busy cleaning some small tables from the night before.

'Coffee, Nan,' he said, without glancing in her direction.

'Right away, sir'. she answered as she left the room.

William picked up a letter from the desk and opened it with a gold knife. He glanced at it briefly before throwing it into the large fireplace. Moving slowly to the full-length window overlooking his estate and gardens, he gazed out at the lovely Irish summer morning.

'Maud,' he shouted, irritably. 'Maud, where are you?'

'Here, William,' Lady Campbell replied in an equally irritable tone as she entered the room. 'What's wrong now?' She moved to the sofa and sat down, picking up yesterday's paper.

'What's wrong today is what is wrong every day,' he growled, marching to the window again. 'This damn government. That's what's wrong.' Maud knew that once her husband was like this there was no point trying to reason with him, so she stayed silent; making him even more cross. 'The economy is failing; the tenants don't want to work for their rent. and now our own government's demanding that we pay them thousands of back taxes just to stay here.' This conversation had been going on for the last year, but Maud gathered that there was more concern in his voice today.

William turned and looked at her. 'We'll have to leave in the next few years, so what's the point in paying that gardener out there to keep a garden that in a few years will be overgrown?' Maud stood up and went to her husband, taking his arm to try and comfort him. 'We could do worse than move back to England, William,' she said with a sigh.

William stared at the garden and, after a long pause, said, 'This miserable island is where my family came from, and now I shall have no choice but to put the pressure on my own tenants; which I didn't want to do, mark my words. It will make me very unpopular, Maud.' He paused, and seemed genuinely sad. 'I shall have no choice.'

The maid brought a silver tray in with a coffee and tea pot and began to place the cups on the table. 'Leave that, Nan. I'll do it,' Sir William snapped.

'Yes, sir,' Nan replied quietly as she quickly left the room.

'Thank you, Nan,' he called after her more gently and turned to make his own coffee.

Maud joined him to pour her own tea. 'You are a good man, William,' she said softly, taking her cup back to the sofa. 'You've been such a good landlord to the locals, compared to so many.'

William joined her on the sofa. 'I know when I start collecting the rents, many of them will not have the money, but I shall have to force them to pay if we wish to stay here another year.' He dropped his head. 'Some of them might lose their homes. I never wanted this to happen, believe me.'

'I know, darling, but they all know the rules.'

William got up. 'Rules? Yes, rules that we English have imposed on my people in their own land, when we have no right to be here!'

Maud finished her tea and stood up. 'I must go to Londonderry today, William. Why don't you join me?' She walked to the door and turned to see her husband looking more troubled than she had ever seen him before.

'No, my love. I must talk to my manager and see what we are to do.'

'Will you be back for dinner tonight? Don't forget we have been invited to Redcastle.' With that she was gone.

William went to the mantelpiece and pulled a cord that rang the servants' bell deep in the heart of the house. A few minutes later John, the estate manager, appeared. 'You rang, sir?'

'Come in, John. We've got some rather unpleasant work to do.' William went over to the large dresser at the back of the room and pulled out a large map of the area.

Thomas woke the next morning to the sound of someone knocking on the front door. He still wasn't sure what had happened, but he was beginning to remember the fishing trip with his dad. He coughed as he sat up, and he still felt pain in his chest. He was about to call his mother when he heard her already open the door, so he moved slowly through the kitchen, the blanket still wrapped around him.

The men at the door spoke quietly to his mother, and he watched her face grow deathly pale.

Suddenly, before anyone could catch her, she collapsed in a heap on the floor. The men quickly lifted her, carrying her gently into the kitchen and placing her in the wicker chair by the fire.

One of the men then turned to Thomas. 'We found your father, Thomas, I'm afraid he has gone from us.' He put his arm kindly around his shoulder. 'I'm really sorry to have to tell you this, Thomas. He and Fergal were not as lucky as you were, son.'

Thomas stared at the man blankly. He heard Mary come in behind the men, crying hard. She ran over to Thomas and hugged him tightly. 'Oh, Thomas what will we do? We've lost both our fathers.' They held each other tightly for a long time.

The men left as Bridget came around and they all sat by the fire for the rest of the day crying and talking about the accident that had claimed Fergal and Patrick. Mary couldn't stop thinking about her dream - that had now come true. However, their troubles were far from over at this point in time.

Many neighbours from miles away came to the two wakes and the two funerals. Both men were held in high regard in the area as they were always helping neighbours in need. Thomas and Mary were surprised at the number of people who came to the funerals, considering they lived in such an isolated area, but news travelled fast from pub to pub.

Thomas could hardly look at anyone when they shook his hand. He still felt that if he had not mentioned to his father about going fishing on his birthday the two men would have waited until the proper fishing season started, with the kinder weather. He didn't know what to do with himself over the next few weeks. He would never go out in a boat again; in fact, he didn't even want to look at the beach or ever see the sea again.

He took the horse out one day and tried to attach the old plough to it, but it was too heavy for him to work on his own, and now too late for sowing any crop anyway. Instead, he walked the horse over to Mary's house where they sat by the stream talking and crying, while the horse grazed on the new grass by the road.

Rose was stronger than Bridget and was already thinking about the future without Fergal. His crops had been planted and were now well on, due to the warm spring. She kept herself busy every day trying to hide the pain from Mary and Martha. Her Christian faith had always helped her to believe that God would always take care of them, but now she was sick inside wondering why God would allow this to happen to them now. One minute she would have peace and the next panic.

She was always the strong one in the house and would always try to encourage Fergal to believe in God. Fergal had always a quiet way about him and never said much when Rose talked about her faith. He just nodded and smiled when questioned. The thought now of having to ask her twenty-year-old daughter to help her run the farm was a weight she could hardly bear. She had always hoped that Mary would go away and find a life of her own in the city.

Rose came over to the stream and put her hand on Thomas's head. 'Ye better be getting home to your ma now, son. She needs you very much.' Thomas looked up at her kind eyes and was grateful that he had a second family to be with. He now realised that life was going to change a lot.

Bridget knew she had to keep going but was afraid to tell anyone, including Thomas, that they had been badly behind with the rent and that the bailiff had met with Patrick, warning him that it was time to pay. She was worried sick but had to be strong since there was no man to bear the burden with her.

Sir William studied the map with his bailiff, Dermot. John made an excuse to be busy at something else, as he didn't want to have anything to do with chasing tenants for rent. Beside the map he had a list of his tenants and details of their rents.

'I'm surprised, sir,' the bailiff said, pointing to the list, 'that there are only six families behind with their rent.' William looked down the list and marked the six with his pencil. Some owed a few shillings while others eight to twelve pounds.

'Who do you think can realistically pay, Dermot?' asked William, alarmed that he was owed such a small amount. He pointed to a name on the list.

'He's no good, sir, his crops failed for the second year in a row and he spends most of his time in the pub running a tab on his drink,' Dermot replied, laughing.

'What about Patrick Sweeney? He owes twelve pounds. How did we let him get to this amount?'

'He has had two bad years at the fishing, my lord, but I heard that this year he's been selling a lot of fish in Moville at a hefty price. I warned him recently that he was behind with his rent.'

'Right, Dermot. I'll leave it up to you.'

He stood up and moved to the door. 'Only collect money from those who you think can pay. If anyone is hiding anything from us, they will already be well aware of the consequences.'

'Ay, sir. I'll see to it right away.'

William went to the front door where his wife was climbing into the carriage. 'Will you not come to the city, William? It's such nice day, and we might just meet some of your friends.'

'Not today, Maud. I need to get some air. I need to think.' The carriage moved off and William went inside the house.

It was a bright sunny morning and Thomas decided that he would once again visit Mary, as he had done every day since the accident. He had just got over the hill and was about to run down the other side when Mary came around the corner.

'I was just on my way over. What brings you here?' he asked, surprised.

'We're going to our favourite spot to look at the sea, Thomas.'

Thomas shook his head and pulled up his shoulders. 'Never Mary. I'll never look at the sea again - ever.'

'You must, Thomas.'

Mary paused and took both his hands, gazing into his sad eyes.

'You must. If you never look at it again you'll spend your life trapped by fear.'

'I killed both our fathers, Mary. If it hadn't been for my birthday they would still be alive.'

'Oh, Thomas, my dear friend, how wrong you are.' She paused and put her arm around his shoulder. 'They lived for the sea. They knew the risks. If it wasn't that day it would have been another.'

'But it was that day, Mary; and they only went for me.'

'No Thomas. I heard my da saying that they would go because the weather was perfect. They had no idea there was a storm coming, just like we would have no idea about today.'

'Fergal noticed the seagulls were crying loudly and had come into land; a sure sign of bad weather.'

'Look at me, Thomas.' Mary pulled herself around in front of him and came close to his face. 'Nothing you did made any difference to that day, and no one knew a storm was coming on such a peaceful day.' She leaned forward and kissed him on the lips and then stood back, not realising what she had just done.

Thomas just stared at her in disbelief for a moment and then looked down in embarrassment. He didn't not know what to say. He felt like he had just been kissed by his sister, and yet it felt like a very special moment. First, he thought it was wrong; then he thought it was right; then he didn't know what to think.

'Why did you do that?'

She stared at him, then lowered her head. 'I don't know, Thomas. It just happened.'

Mary took him by the hand and led him down the path to the beach. They sat down at their usual spot and stared out at the blue sea and said nothing. Thomas could only stare at the horizon. Looking down at the beach where the boat used to be kept was still too difficult.

'My da lived for us, Mary,' Thomas said, sadly. 'He was the kindest man God ever put on this earth.'

'My da was the same, Thomas,' Mary said, holding his hand, 'but they both would be annoyed if we didn't live to help our families now.'

'What help can we be in this lonely forsaken place Mary?' Thomas sighed standing up. 'How can I work for my family when there isn't anything to do here?'

Just then, they were both shaken out of their sad reflections by a man calling Thomas from the top of the hill. 'Who's that?' said Mary, trying to see the stranger. 'Come on. We'd better go, Thomas.' She grabbed his hand again and pulled him up the hill. The man met them near the corner and he was out of breath.

'Are you Thomas?' he asked, Thomas noticing the urgency in his voice.

'Yes sir' replied Thomas apprehensively.

'Sir William's bailiff has just now put your mother out of the house! She's in a terrible state'! You need to run home quickly, Thomas!'

Thomas let go of Mary's hand and raced back over the hill to his house. He could see three men on large black horses turning out of his yard. One of them threw a lit torch onto the thatched roof and it immediately caught fire. The last rider saw Thomas running towards him and halted his horse while the others rode on. 'Let other tenants know this is what happens when you don't pay your rent,' Dermot the bailiff shouted back.

Thomas stopped, transfixed, staring at the house. He could see his mother was sitting by the wall with her head in her hands crying, but unharmed. A strange bolt of courage grabbed him, and he shouted after the man. 'You tell Sir William that this day he has taken my mother's house but that someday I will watch him being evicted from his! Mark my words.' The bailiff stopped and turned the horse to look sneeringly at Thomas.

'I wish you well, young fool. You will need an army with you when you come.' He laughed and rode away.

Thomas ran to his mother and held her in his arms. 'It's all right, Ma. It's all right.'

It wasn't long before Mary and the neighbour arrived, and all of them stood and watched the roof of the cottage burn until it was gone. The bailiff had allowed Bridget to get her possessions out of the house before they burnt it. It was a sorry sight. Thomas looked at Mary and stared into her eyes as if he were saying goodbye. How could life change so much so quickly? He was now a man, and he suddenly felt a huge burden of responsibility upon him.

He stood up as he saw Rose running up the lane with Martha holding her hand. She stopped a few feet away and looked at the house, horrified. She stood staring at Bridget and Thomas for a few minutes, but then suddenly sprang decisively into action.

'Right now, Bridget and Thomas. Grab your things,' she said, as she picked up a wooden box of food that had been rescued from the kitchen. 'Come with me.'

'What are you doing, Rose?' cried Bridget, through her tears.'

'You have no house of your own. Now you will live with me,' she announced firmly. Thomas looked at Mary and dropped his eyes to the ground. 'No arguing. That's it done,' she said, grabbing Bridget and pulling her up.

'No Rose. I'm not going anywhere. We'll be fine.' Bridget protested.

'Oh, you'll be fine all right, Bridget, once you are in our house,' scolded Rose.

There was no more arguing as Rose barked out instructions to everyone as to what to carry. She told the neighbour to go and fetch the cart to bring any farming equipment that was still working over to the house.

Chapter 4

Sir William and Lady Campbell dismounted from the carriage at the front door of the manor and gave instructions to the driver. They were about to enter the front door when they heard three black horses approaching, so they waited.

'First eviction complete, Sir William,' Dermot said, pleased with himself, but reluctantly added, 'the woman gave me some sad story about her husband being drowned a few weeks ago - and there was no money.'

'Who was that tenant?' asked Sir William, with a stern look on his face.

'Bridget Sweeney, sir.' William walked to the horse. 'And what did you do?'

The bailiff knew something was wrong and began to get a bit nervous. 'I put the Sweeney woman outside and torched the house, sir.'

'Did I tell you to do that?' Sir William was now shaking with rage. 'Were not my instructions to only evict people as a last resort? I never told you to burn the house, bailiff! It would have been better for you to have enquired locally first about the woman's husband. He was drowned just two weeks ago, you say? Didn't you even bother to enquire locally whether or not she was telling the truth?'

The bailiff now looked very nervous. 'I didn't know, sir. I only did what is being done by the other landlords. I thought you would be pleased.'

'Pleased?' he shouted, furiously. 'I'll only be pleased when you and your henchmen leave my property! That was a despicable act of cruelty! Besides, how can we ever be accepted by the local people now?'

Lady Campbell walked over to her husband and grabbed him, 'Come inside William. It's done. It can't be changed now.' William marched into the house in a rage while Maud motioned to the men that it was better that they leave straight away.

'I only wanted tenants evicted as a last resort, and only if there was somewhere else for them to live. I didn't expect this!' shouted Sir William as his wife entered the living room. 'We are not like the other landlords and we never will be, mark my words!'

'They were only doing what they thought was right,' Lady Campbell said soothingly in a vain attempt to calm her husband down.

'Right. But all my time here I've tried not to misuse the Irish in their own land. I've done my best to make sure all my staff are well looked after and that the locals think we are not the worst in the world. Now what do we do? How can we even set foot in any village or town without being shunned - or even killed?'

'We could let people know it was a mistake dear.'

'Mistake? Then, mocking sarcastically: ' "Oh dear, I'm very sorry, I got my bailiff to evict a woman and her son who had just been bereaved and then burnt their cottage, but it's all right now. It was just a mistake'. He went over to his desk and, in a temper, ripped the map and tenant list, throwing them in the fire. 'I would rather go to ruin myself than do any more of this work, Maud.'

Lady Campbell slipped out the door, knowing it would be better to leave him for the rest of the day. She knew this meant trouble ahead, but now it was nearly dinner time.

Sir William rang the bell for John his estate manager. 'You rang, sir?' John asked, coming into the drawing room.

'Yes. John will you please make sure that Dermot my bailiff has left the premises and then come back to me and see me. We must devise a plan to save our estate.' John left and Sir William sank into his deep soft chair.

Big adjustments were happening in Rose's cottage to make room for the new arrivals. Fergal had been left money and land from his parents and he built the cottage at the time they got married. It wasn't a typical Donegal cottage since most houses at the time in Donegal had only two or three rooms, whereas Fergal had extended the length of his to include a kitchen, living room and four bedrooms, with an out-house built on at the end. Like all the other cottages in Ireland it was thatched. However, Fergal had insisted in getting one of Ireland's top thatchers to do the roof, which meant it was well insulated. Rose had a room to herself, as did Bridget, while Mary and Martha now shared. Thomas was left with the smallest room to himself.

Life became busy in the summer as the crops had to be harvested, not to mention the turf on the bog that they owned a mile away on the mountain. They all tried to make work compensate for the pain they were feeling, but many days at least one of them would break down and cry. Thomas was having to adjust to being the only man in the house, and at times he felt the responsibility was too much for him. He still wanted to be free and dreamed of having a real job with a home of his own.

After a long day on the bog, where they stacked the turf ready to come home in the cart, Thomas sat down overlooking the long beach on the other side of Lough Foyle. Mary sat down beside him rubbing her brown turf-coloured hands on the grass. 'I suppose we're stuck here now, Mary,' he sighed wistfully. 'This is it then.' She didn't reply, but gently put her arm around him and laid her head on his shoulder. 'I asked you before why you kissed me, but I never got any reply,' he ventured, still staring out at Benone Strand.

'I don't know,' Mary said wistfully.

'It felt strange - but nice.'

Mary blushed and felt uneasy.

'It was something I just wanted to do. I didn't even think about it.'

'Would you do it again?' he asked, smiling at her.

'I might.' She jumped to her feet. 'You never know what way the wind blows,' she said playfully. With that she was off, running down the bog track with Thomas after her.

'I was in Moville today,' said Rose, as they all gathered round the table for dinner. 'Everyone was talking about the number of people who are getting the ship from Londonderry to America.'

There was silence. 'It seems a lot of people are getting work there and earning good money.'

Thomas looked at Mary with longing eyes. She knew from their long chats by the sea that Thomas wanted to go to America and become somebody. They had heard before of families leaving, and had discussed the issue many times. He would like to fulfil his father's dream and become an engineer. He dreamed of designing machines that would make life easier on the farm and other things. Mary had said she would like to make fabulous clothes instead of the dreary ones that everyone wore in Ireland.

Neither said anything to Rose but smiled at each other across the table. The smile was seen by Bridget, who wondered how long these two young lovers would stay to look after their mothers.

She put some more meat and potatoes on Thomas's plate and then, right out of the blue, she announced, 'I'm thinking, Thomas, it's time to sell the horse.' Thomas dropped his fork with a clang on the plate. 'What, Ma?'

'He's nearly done, son, and we don't want the burden of feeding him in winter again.'

Thomas looked alarmed, but he knew she was right and it would be more of a burden on Rose.

'There is a fair on in Moville tomorrow. Maybe you could see if anyone would want the nag.' Thomas didn't answer for he knew that this was one more challenge that he had to deal with.

After dinner, Mary and Thomas sat at the front of the house on the old wooden seat. The sun sank slowly over the soft Irish hills. 'This is a great place to live Mary, so why do I dream of leaving all the time? It's as if I was born with a spirit to torment me that somewhere over that sunset lies a better life.'

Mary put her arm through his. 'Maybe there is, Thomas, but maybe it's not the right time. Only God knows.'

'What has God got to do with it Mary? he laughed.

'Do you not believe in God, Thomas?' Mary looked concerned.

'I don't really know. All I know about God is what I heard from the priest on a Sunday whenever Ma would drag me to chapel. That's it.'

'My ma always brought me up to know God in a very personal way; not just in church.'

Thomas turned and looked at her intently with sadness in his voice. 'Well this personal God has not done a big lot for us this summer, has he?'

'He has done more than you know, Thomas. He saved your life.'

'Yes, and took both our fathers away,' he replied, cynically.

'Well, Thomas. We are born, and we die. That time is appointed for us. Some live long lives, some live short, but we just have to make the best of the time that we are given.' Thomas looked away and sighed. Right now, he didn't know what he believed any more.

'Will ye come with me to Moville tomorrow?' he asked, with a pleading tone.

'I would love to, but I promised Martha we would go crab fishing on the beach tomorrow before the summer ends.' The sun went down, and they returned to the kitchen for tea.

Chapter 5

It was a long walk over the mountain track with the horse the next day, and Thomas thought a few times that the old nag wouldn't make it. It did, and to his surprise, someone offered him three pounds for the horse at the fair. He and Rose had set a limit of two pounds, so he could hardly believe his luck.

Moville was very busy with horses, carts and carriages coming and going down the main street. He walked past some of the shops and was amazed at some of the things for sale that he had never seen before - and the noise! People were shouting and waving, and everyone seemed to be in a jovial mood. 'I could get used to this,' he thought, as he made his way back up the street out of the town.

Just then, someone called him, and he turned to see a man with a hat and a pipe who had been watching him. 'You were lucky to sell that horse today, son. Did you know who bought it?' Thomas shrugged his shoulders. He thought this was a strange question.

'Campbell's man,' the man announced, obviously disapprovingly.

'Which Campbell?' Thomas replied, now interested.

'Sir William Campbell. The man who burnt your house.' The man was obviously enjoying this latest bit of gossip. Thomas suddenly felt sick, then angry. He wanted to go back and take it from him but knew his ma needed the money.

'But, did you hear he sacked the bailiff who burnt your house? He was not at all pleased with him,' added the pipe-smoking man. Thomas felt like thumping something in his anger, but he resisted. He needed to control himself now. He was a man. He just turned and hurried towards the village of Greencastle.

As he got to the top of the hill, his own bog on the left and the spectacular view of the sea on the right, he spied a stranger in the distance. He was holding a pole with a circle on top and was dressed in the most unusual, expensive looking clothes he had ever seen. He wore a hat that had peak on the front and back and the green jacket matched the trousers.

As Thomas got closer he noticed that he was mumbling to himself as he looked through the circle on the pole. He stopped and watched him from a little way off. The man picked up another pole and walked two hundred yards to a height to the right of the road. He tried to hammer the second pole into the ground, but it fell over several times before fixing it in the ground with a heavy clout. He looked up as he noticed Thomas watching him curiously, but continued working. Then he went back to the first pole, continuing to look through the circle. Now the first pole fell over, and the man cursed with a strange accent.

'Do you want a job, boy?' the stranger called to Thomas.

Thomas stood and looked at him thinking he might be a little deranged.

'I will pay you money if you hold this damn pole.' The man's face was red, and Thomas thought he was genuinely exhausted by what he was doing. After hesitating for a minute, his conviction about helping strangers got the better of him and he went and picked up the pole.

'Hold it very straight, son' the man shouted as he looked through the circle on the first pole.

'To the left,' he called again. 'No, not that much. Slightly to the right. That way, that way. Hold it still now, son.' The man took out a long tape with numbers on it and walked slowly towards Thomas, counting under his breath until he got close to him.

'Good lad, good lad,' he smiled.' I've been trying to do that for the last half hour.'

The stranger shook Thomas by the hand. 'Thank you. My name's Charles - and you are?'

'Thomas. Sir, do you mind if I ask you something? What are you doing?' The man laughed.

'I come from England, and I'm working on the first ordnance survey map of Ireland. My valued partner took ill a few days ago and now I am left to finish this job on my own.' He gathered up the two poles and the rest of his equipment he had in a bag. 'I think that'll do me for one day,' he puffed, as he wrote down figures on a map.

Thomas was about to continue home when the man suddenly turned to him and asked. 'Would you like a job for a few days, son? I could pay you two shillings a day.' That sounded like a lot to Thomas. He was taken aback by his generous offer.

'What would I have to do, sir?'

'Just what you've done, but it would be all day.' The man put his hand in his pocket then handed Thomas one shilling. 'We'll call that a down payment for tomorrow then.' He had a kind, jolly face and Thomas felt he could trust him.

'Where will I come, sir?'

'Just meet me at the bottom of that hill over there at seven AM, and you don't need to call me "Sir" he laughed. You may call me "Charles".

'Right Sir. I'll be there tomorrow at seven then.' The man turned and headed back towards Greencastle. Thomas walked on, trying to figure out was what just happened. Was this real?'

Thomas could hardly contain his excitement as he explained to everyone back at the cottage that he had been given a paid job. He handed Rose the money and said there would be more of that to come by the end of the week. Everyone wanted to know where the man came from and what he was doing, but Thomas could remember little of what the man had said. He could only remember that he was a little overweight, pleasant, and dressed in strange clothes; someone who talked to himself and held poles for measuring heights and hollows in the ground. Rose and Bridget were somewhat concerned but were prepared to let him go back the next day to see how he would get on. Mary suggested that she might go with him just to see if he was genuine, but Thomas was certain he was capable of doing this on his own.

The next morning, Thomas met the Englishman at the bottom of the Greencastle side of the mountain. He was waiting for him by a rusty gate with a cow looking over his shoulder, still smoking his pipe and talking to himself.

'My ma wants to know what "ordnance survey" is, sir'

'Twelve years ago, a team of us surveyors came over to map Ireland since the government had no proper records of the land in this country. This is my last four days and my part of the survey will be complete. I will be travelling home on Saturday. My partner took sick last week and has already gone back to England. If you hadn't shown up I was going to have to invent figures and draw a map on what I think instead of what I see.' He gave a big laugh and patted Thomas on the back. 'But now, son, since I have you, the government will have an accurate map of this wild part of Donegal and everyone will be very happy, including me. Soon I will get home to see my family.'

'And what does that pole do?' asked Thomas, picking up the pole that had a measuring device on the top of it.

'By looking through this machine at the other pole that you hold I can measure distance and height, and when I bring all these numbers back to head office they can then make an accurate map out of my drawing. 'Now listen, lad.' He turned and picked up his bag. 'We have many miles to cover today and I shall explain everything as we go along.'

'Right, Sir,' said Thomas, picking up the other pole.

'And if you call me "Sir" one more time I shall be forced to send you home,' he laughed. 'My name is Charles, and "Charles" it will be all day.'

Thomas was about to say, "Yes, Sir" again but managed to mutter a hesitant, "Yes, Charles".'

The day was long as Charles had said, and they covered nearly five miles right down to the village when the light started to fade. Thomas was tired, but now he was going to have to walk home again over the mountain track in the dark. Just then a local man came by with a horse and cart.

'Young Thomas,' the man shouted. 'you're a long way from home at this time of the night. Hop up into my cart.' Thomas ran to the cart, scarcely taking time to say good bye to Charles.

'Same time this spot in the morning, lad,' Charles called after him as he climbed into the back of the cart.

'Right, sir', and with that they were off.

When they had travelled half a mile up the track the man turned to him had asked in a rough tone. 'Why were you speaking to an Englishman. boy?'

'I'm working for him,' replied Thomas, now recognising him as being one of the men that had carried him from the shore.

'We don't work for the English, Thomas. They come over here and steal our land, our houses, our animals and then leave to go home rich.' Thomas didn't know what to say so he stayed silent.

'He's probably working for that man who put your roof in. Take my advice, son, and stay well away. You don't need his money.' Thomas knew that Charles was not like that, but he also knew that trying to persuade this man was not going to happen, so he lay down on the straw and went to sleep.

Chapter 6

Sir William couldn't sleep, so he slipped out of the bed without waking Maud. He had to get the early morning air as the financial strain of the estate was getting to him.

William had sent one of his farm workers to see if there was a small cottage in which he could re-house Bridget and Thomas, but there were none vacant. He wanted to go and visit them but knew it might make things worse. He knew that other landlords in Ireland were involved in regular evictions, but that didn't make it right. He longed to return home to England, and was annoyed that he had given in to pressure from a government official to move to this huge new estate in Ireland.

The servants were not up yet so he went down to the kitchen and made his own tea before going out the back door to the stables. He had sent one of his farm workers into Moville to buy a good ploughing horse and the man had landed back with an old mare that only had one or two years to live. Just then, upon turning the corner, William was horrified! He could see smoke and flames coming from the stables, and the horses were making a terrifying noise.

'Oh, dear God,' he shouted as he ran to try and open the door, but the flames beat him back.

'John! John!' he yelled back at the house. 'Fire! Fire!'

Within a few minutes, John, the estate manager, appeared, still in his night shirt, but wearing boots. He tried to help William get the door open, but the fire was too well advanced. They both ran to another shed and got steel buckets, which they filled from the pump. They tried throwing buckets of water at the fire, which did prevent it from spreading to the main house but, sadly, the stables were gone.

The local fire brigade arrived half an hour later when the fire was nearly out, and they proceeded to clear up some of the mess.

William sat on a barrel with his head buried in his hands, tears flowing down his blackened cheeks. 'All my horses John, all my horses,' he cried. John didn't know what to say so he just stood quietly beside him, face to the ground, knowing that the horses were William's pride and joy.

A short while later the chief of the fire service approached William, carrying a steel can. 'Sir William, it seems that your fire was no accident.' He paused, seeing William stand up. 'We found this can of paraffin by the door.' William sank back down onto the barrel and closed his eyes.

'I'm very sorry about your animals, sir. If someone had called us earlier, we may have been able to save them.'

'It's not your fault, chief.' replied William. 'They were gone long before you got here.'

'I will be reporting this to the sergeant in Moville, sir. We need to catch the men who did this.'

'Thank you, gentlemen,' said William, as he walked back to the house.

Maud met him at the door and tried to hug him, but he brushed her aside and stomped in, slamming the door shut.

That evening Sir William and Maud had invited friends for a dinner party, which they decided should go ahead since William wanted to ask advice of his friends. The party should have been a night of fine food, wine and music, but instead of fun and laughter, the mood was somber since most people had heard about the fire.

'Shocking business, Willie,' said Colonel Dewhurst, downing a glass of whiskey after a very quiet dinner party.

'Not sure what to do now, old chap,' replied William, lighting his cigar. 'I suppose we should be grateful it was the stable and not the house they tried to burn.'

'Hmm, they might try again Willie.'

'Yes, I know, Dew. The local police are hunting them down and providing us with a guard at the gate.'

'I was surprised to hear that you destroyed the peasant's cottage Willie. That's a little out of character for you.'

'It wasn't,' replied William coldly. 'It was my damn bailiff. I would never have done that to anyone.'

Colonel Dewhurst came up close to William. 'My advice, Willie, is to let everyone know that it was not your decision and let the bailiff take the blame. I believe he has fled the area, anyway. I would say most local people who know you would accept that once they hear it from yourself. It might calm things down.'

'My grandfather came to Scotland from this land, and I shall never forget that I am half Irish and half Scottish. If we go far enough back, we are all related, and I hate our inherent snobbery in thinking the Irish are people are here to serve us.' Colonel Dewhurst went quiet and looked at the floor, thinking quickly how he might change the subject. William turned to his other guests and thanked them for coming as most wanted to leave early anyhow.

Thomas enjoyed the next two days as there was much less walking now since most of the surveying was around Greencastle Fort and village. Every time they were measuring a piece of ground Charles would shout instructions to Thomas to move right or left or back or forwards. Thomas couldn't understand or hear Charles most times, so he suggested that they use hand signals. At first Charles thought this was unnecessary and continued to shout, but by the end of the week he was using the signals as he was tired of shouting.

'You are a very clever young lad and will go far, son,' he said, as handed Thomas his shilling. 'I wish I had someone like you in England. It would make my life a lot easier.'

'Thank you, Charles,' he said, rubbing the coin. 'Will you need me tomorrow?'

'Yes, lad, last day tomorrow. We have very little to do, so off home with you and get some well-earned sleep.'

Thomas was sad walking home as he had begun to enjoy the work very much. He found that Charles was one of nicest and kindest men he had ever met. He wondered how he could ever go back to farm work next week - and that with no money, as well. Mary was waiting at the gate for him when he hobbled down the lane. 'You look tired Thomas,' she said, laughing. 'Is real work too hard for you?'

'No real work isn't too hard for me, Mary, but it does involve a lot of walking.' 'Tomorrow is my last day, and I don't want it to end.'

Mary put her arm round his shoulder. 'Come in, Thomas. I kept you some stew. Our mothers are away down the road to visit Pat and his family.'

Thomas and Mary talked for hours about what life must be like in other parts of the world. They both shared the same dream of leaving Donegal for a better life.

When Thomas came down the hill into Greencastle the next morning he was surprised to see that Charles was not waiting at the place they had agreed to meet. He walked further down the narrow road till he came to the main road that led to Moville. He looked in both directions but no sign of Charles. He stood and waited by the gable end of a thatched cottage but there was no one awake yet in the village. His heart sank at the thought of Charles having left without even saying goodbye. He turned to walk back the way he had come when Charles came running up the road behind him.

'Thomas!' he called. He was puffed and even more red in the face than usual. 'Thomas, listen, son. I was looking for you,' he panted. 'I've some bad news for you, lad.' Thomas looked at him in silence as he was getting used to bad news by now. He wondered what was coming next.

'I've got to go now, Thomas. I got the dates wrong, and my ship leaves Belfast tomorrow, which means I've got to catch the coach from Londonderry today. I will have to make up today's figures. Thomas still just stood and stared at him. His first paid job had now come to an abrupt end.

Charles held out his hand and put a shilling into Thomas' hand. 'That's for the day that I promised you, son. You're a great young man. I shall miss you.'

Thomas felt tears welling up in his eyes and he dropped his head. 'I want to thank you, Charles, for your kindness to me. I wish I was going with you.'

Charles looked at him intensely, painfully aware that the young boy in front of him would have a totally wasted life on a farm. He was one of the cleverest young people he had ever come across and, in a moment of complete spontaneity he suddenly blurted, 'Would you like to come and work for me in England, Thomas?' Thomas was shocked, and whole ream of emotions surged through his body.

'England, sir? That far away!'

'Yes. It's true, it's very far, Thomas, but I would pay you very well; maybe even three shillings a day once you are trained right.' Thomas moved nervously and didn't know what to say. 'There's one big problem, though, Thomas.' Charles grabbed his two arms and held them. 'The coach from Moville to Londonderry leaves in four hours.' He paused. 'I would really love you to come, but there's very little time to say goodbye to your folks. You need to go now!'

'I don't know, sir,' Thomas stammered. 'I don't know if my ma could manage without me.'

'It's up to you, son, but I must go now and get ready.' He turned and began walking down the road and called back, "Whatever you decide - I'll be at the main road in four hours.' Thomas watched him walk about one hundred yards and he felt sick in his stomach for what he was about to do. He looked back up the mountain and whispered something, then turned and ran after Charles. He was out of breath when he caught up with him.

'Two shillings a day?' he checked. 'Yes, son, and three shillings a day after training. You'll be able to send a lot of money home every month as we'll give you a place to live free.'

'I'm coming then, Charles.' Thomas ran back over the mountain as if his life depended on it. How would they all react to him deciding to do what he had always dreamed of? It was unthinkable that this was, at last, becoming a reality!

Rose and Bridget were busy dusting an old rug by the front door and Mary was helping Martha feed the chickens when Thomas arrived, out of breath. 'What's wrong, Thomas?' Mary asked, alarmed at the speed at which he came running up the lane. Thomas stopped and bent down to get his breath.

'The Englishman has asked me to go with him to his own country to work for him full time,' he blurted out. trying to avoid their gaze. 'I said I would. It will give us all enough money to stay here and live for the rest of our lives.' There was silence. 'The only problem is, I have to leave now to catch the next coach with him.' Thomas tried to hide his excitement.

The silence was broken only when Mary walked over to him and gazed his eyes, whispering something inaudible into his ear. 'I don't know what to do Mary,' he cried. 'I can't leave you, but I'll never get a chance like this ever again.'

'I'll really miss you, Thomas, but if God has opened a door for you then you should go.' Her tears were welling up but still managed to stroke the hair out of his eyes. Thomas look sadly at his family. 'I want to look after everyone, but I just can't do it here.' His mother came over and put her arm around his shoulder. 'Go Thomas, we'll be fine.'

Rose came over and stood with her arms crossed. 'It's God's provision for you and us, Thomas.' She paused and with a sigh said resignedly, 'We don't know what lies ahead for this land, but it isn't looking good lad, and none of us want you to go to sea like our men. This will break our hearts, but we know it's the right thing to do.'

'I have to get my things now,' Thomas said, sadly, through his tears.

'I'll help you,' Mary answered, grabbing his arm and pulling him into the house. They quickly stuffed a few clean clothes into a bag and Mary grabbed a St. Bridget's cross that she had made years before. She stopped packing and handed it to Thomas.

'One day I will come back and marry you, Mary,' he surprised her by announcing, tucking the cross into his shirt. 'When I've made enough money to keep us here, I'll come back and marry you.' He repeated.

'Thank you, my love.' Mary leant forward and kissed him hard on the lips and they both hugged each other tightly. She was crying now. 'You'd better, Thomas, or I'll come looking for you,' she whispered, trying to muster up her usual playfulness through her tears. She grabbed his bag and pushed him out the door. 'God be with you and bring you home to me again.'

Bridget and Rose hugged him at the door, trying hard not to reveal their sadness. Thomas went over to Martha who was still by the gate with the chickens. 'Goodbye, sweet Martha,' he said, touching her smiling face. 'Have a good day,' she replied, laughing, oblivious to the fact that she may not see him for a very long time. With that, he was gone.

Thomas felt sick with sadness as he ran back over the mountain and thought of slowing down so that he would miss the coach. The walk from Greencastle to Moville took them less than an hour and they made the coach in good time. Thomas had never seen a coach before, let alone travelled in one, and he was amazed at how shiny and clean everything was. The seats were blue velvet and there were glass windows and doors with leather trim on the inside. He sat back and watched the beauty of Lough Foyle on his left, wondering what new life lay before him.

Charles sat facing him and now wondered if he had done the right thing. He would have to convince his manager that Thomas was worth taking on - and that he hadn't kidnapped him! He stared at him now and thought of his family who were going to miss him so very much. He suddenly felt nervous, and thought about letting him go back on the next coach.

'How old are you, Thomas?' he asked, out of the blue.

Thomas paused for a second, and then lied. 'Twenty-one, Charles.'

'Who's at home?'

'My ma and some friends.'

'Friends?'

'Yes. We lost our house recently and now we live with friends. An Englishman put us out of our house.' He suddenly realised what he had just said and was about to apologise. Charles sat back on the soft seat, looking sadly at Thomas. He decided not to ask any more.

Thomas felt sick. 'What was he doing? Where exactly was he going? What about Mary?' He panicked and thought about jumping out of the coach. He then thought of the conversation he had with Mary about leaving Donegal for better things - and for three shillings a day! He could send his ma home over three pounds a month and it would mean they wouldn't have to worry anymore. Mary could join him, and maybe they could get married - but then he panicked again.

The view of the Foyle changed to fields and then an occasional house. They were nearly in the city. The carriage speeded up as the road improved, and soon they were passing a harbour with rows of ships. Hundreds of people were walking up and down the quay. Some were waving at passengers already on the ships and some were carrying heavy bundles on their backs with lots of children in tow.

'People leaving for America, Thomas.' Charles said, as he watched Thomas's eyes grew bigger. 'Everyone in your land is looking for a new life.'

The coach came to a halt and a man in a uniform came over and opened the door. 'Londonderry,' he shouted. 'All change here for Belfast, Dublin and Sligo.' Thomas and Charles jumped out while the driver threw Charles his bag from the back of the coach.

'I'll buy you tea,' said Charles as walked towards a small tea room. 'It'll be a very long journey to Belfast, son. We'll have many stops along the way.'

Thomas was in shock at the new world he had set foot in. He had never seen so many people, dressed in such fancy clothes! They all looked very important, but no one looked at him in the eye.

The air was heavy with a smoke he had never smelled before. He was used to the gentle smell of turf burning in the kitchen, but this smoke tasted bitter and it made his throat dry. There were so many carriages going up and down the main street of Londonderry, as well as carts pulled by two horses full of goods he had never seen before.

Charles looked at him, noticing how new all this to him, and was now really regretting having asked him to come. New life maybe was not this best idea for him after all. 'Thomas, I could put you on the next coach home if you like, son. Maybe that would be for the best.'

'No, sir,' he replied as they walked into the tea room. 'This is amazing, and I know my friend Mary will like it too some day.' Charles looked at him curiously but said nothing. They found a small wooden table, and a young girl in a uniform placed two cups down on the table, taking from the fire place a large kettle from which she poured hot tea. 'It's a very long journey to Belfast, Thomas. You need to eat some of that fresh Irish bread,' said Charles, as he used a sharp knife to cut off four slices of bread. 'I still think I should put you on the next coach home. Your mother will blame me for taking you away.' He kept worrying that the local people would think he had kidnapped the boy.

'What Englishman put you out of your house, Thomas?' Charles ventured gently, sipping his tea. Thomas didn't want to answer as he felt uncomfortable talking about this subject with another Englishman.

'He owned our house, sir, and when my father drowned, my ma couldn't pay the rent.'

'Hmm,' Charles mused, and Thomas noted a look of compassion his eyes.

'Eat up now, son. We'll be on our way soon..'.

Chapter 7

Sir William was up early the next morning for breakfast on his own. He hadn't slept well all night thinking about what he was going to do and how the locals might react. Lady Campbell had heard him get up and went down to the dining room in her dressing gown. 'Why are you up so early, William?' The sun is the only thing up before you!'

He finished his mouthful of eggs and wiped his chin with the white napkin. 'I'm going to go and visit the family I evicted, Maud, and I'm going to offer them a new house.' Maud looked at him, horrified.

'Do you really think that's a good idea William? They might even attack you!'

'I have no choice,' he replied sternly, rising from the table. 'I refuse to have my name associated with such a cruel deed. We may be regarded as English landlords, but we are still human, and one day we might lose our own roof if we cannot raise the money our own government is asking us for.' William rang the bell for John.

'You rang, sir?'

'Yes, John. Get me a horse from somewhere – hold on - get me two. We're going on a journey.'

'I took the liberty, my lord, of buying three horses yesterday to replace the ones that got burnt in the fire. I hope I did the right thing as I thought you and my lady would be needing transport.'

William began to get angry with him for spending estate money without permission, but then thought better of it. He said quietly, looking out the window, 'Good man, John. You did right.'

Sir William and John set off an hour later as it was beginning to rain. 'Do you know where the family live now. John?' he asked, as they turned out of the gate of the estate.

'I believe they all live together now in a house about a mile from their old one. There are very few houses in that area, so we should find them, sir.' They turned right onto the coach road for Moville. Mary and two men came walking towards them. They stopped the horses twenty yards away as the walkers approached them.

'I'm looking for a Bridget Sweeney and Rose Doherty,' shouted William.

'And who are you?' replied one of the men, in a slightly threatening voice.

'I'm Sir William Campbell.'

'Have you come to take the roof off her house again?' The man sneered.

'No. I have come to give her a new home.'

The man squared his shoulders up and grabbed a long stick from the hedge. 'They don't need a new house from the likes of you. Go on home - before I send you home for good!' John walked his horse over to the man and estimated that he could easily defend William if either of them tried to attack.

'It wasn't Sir William who put the roof in of Sweeney's house. It was his bailiff - who has now gone. Sir William never sanctioned it and he was very annoyed when he found out about it. He has always treated his tenants well and is very sorry for what has happened.' There was silence among the group.

'Are you connected to that man Thomas Sweeney has gone to work for?' asked Mary.

'Who is Thomas Sweeney?' Sir William enquired.

'He's the son of the woman you put out of her house,'

'I have no one local who has joined my staff, miss.'

Mary and the two men stood in silence before Mary said in a quieter voice 'We don't need your new house, sir, or your charity, but would only ask you to find out where our Thomas has gone. We're all worried about him.'

'You mentioned he went with an Englishman. When was this?'

'Only yesterday morning,' answered one of the men, 'and no harm had better come to him.'

'I shall make enquiries for you.' William replied, glad of an opportunity to try to be seen to help, at least. With that William and John turned their horses and headed back to his estate.

'I heard from locals that there was a man from the ordnance survey company working in this area for the last few months. Maybe the young lad has gone with him,' said John.

'Maybe, John, but I would like to find out for sure,' William sighed. 'This family have suffered enough.'

Thomas was getting very tired of the coach since the view was pretty boring with mile after mile of flat green fields on each side of the road. They would stop at every village where parcels would be loaded onto the back of the coach. Two more travellers got on at the village of Dungiven that morning, which made it very crushed and uncomfortable inside. He had lost count of the number of times the coachman had stopped and changed the horses at stables and inns along the road. He tried to sleep, but the others were chatting so much that they kept waking him up.

It was getting dark as the coach stopped by the harbour in Belfast to allow the sea travellers off at their boat. Thomas was so tired. He was excited about going on a ship, but was very glad when Charles showed him into a tiny cabin with two beds in it. He just lay down and fell fast asleep.

Thomas woke up with a start with Charles calling him for breakfast. 'When does, the ship leave Charles?' he asked sleepily.

'We're coming into Liverpool already, lad.' Charles laughed. 'You slept through a fairly rough crossing.' He put on his tweed jacket. 'Come on, young fella, till I show you what a good English breakfast is like.'

Thomas followed him out the cabin door down a long dimly lit corridor to a flight of stairs. At the top of the stairs they went down another corridor which led into a room which was full of tables with dirty dishes. They had just made it in time as most passengers had eaten their breakfast and were getting ready to disembark.

'Eat up, son. We have a long train journey ahead of us. No more of your horse-drawn coaches, now,' he said, laughing.

'Where are we going?' asked Thomas, casually, even though it made no difference to him.

'Southampton, Thomas. To our new office. Our office in London had a fire, so we have a new one down by the sea. It's wonderful. You can watch all the big ships sailing off to many parts of the world.'

Charles helped him to his feet and they made their way out of the ship. Thomas's eyes got bigger and bigger as he tried to take in all the sights at the harbour. With so much going on he felt almost dizzy. They boarded a first-class compartment on the steam train waiting by the harbour, and as they got in a whistle blew and the train started to move.

'That was close, lad. Any more breakfast and we would have missed our train.' The train passed through miles and miles of houses and factories as it slowly pulled away from Liverpool until at last there was just endless green. It was cool for October and there wasn't much heat on the train. Charles reached up above the seat to a storage rack and pulled down a blanket to put round Thomas's shoulders.

'So, what would you like to do in life, Thomas?'

'I want to make enough money to return to my home and make sure my ma and friends are well looked after for life.'

'That's a good idea, lad, but have you thought how you would make all this money?'

'All my life I think of making things work better - like showing you signals for your poles instead of shouting. I used to suggest ways of making things easier for my da in his boat.' He went silent again and dropped his head as all the fond memories of his father came flooding back to him.

'I'll mention this to my boss when we get to the office. It might help persuade him to let you stay. If you stick at this job for a few years, son, you could end up being a foreman and earning lots of money.' Thomas looked alarmed and suddenly felt very homesick at the thought of being away from home for a few years.

Sir William and John entered the gates of the estate near tea time. Someone in Moville told them that they had seen a man and a boy get on the Londonderry coach yesterday morning and that they seemed to be in a hurry. 'If that was the ordnance survey man he was working for then he must be heading back to England. We need to use our contacts there to find them before something bad happens to the lad,' Sir William said as they reached the front door.

'I would hardly think he has kidnapped him, my lord. More likely he just persuaded him to go with him to work,' replied John, dismounting and holding William's horse.

'Nevertheless, we must do all we can, John. I'll send some telegrams in the morning. Thank you for your help today.'

'You're welcome, Sir. I'm sure it'll all work out well in the end,' he said, with less confidence than he felt.

William entered the front door while John led the horses around to shed at the back. Maud was in the library reading a book when William came in. 'Well, how did that go, William?' she sighed, putting the book to one side.

'Not as I expected. I think I've made peace with them by promising to try and find their son, though. He may have gone off to England.'

'Not more sadness for that family!' she murmured, moving over to join her husband in a drink from the cocktail bar.'

'Well. I think the Englishman who has been doing the ordnance survey has taken him back to work with him.'

'That's a bit odd, isn't it?' Maud sounded alarmed.

'Yes, it is, and I don't like the sound of it at all. It may be very innocent or, God forbid, something awful. I'll telegram friends I know in Southampton in the morning and see what they come up with, but you know, he's very young - only eighteen.'

'Did you promise them a new house?'

'Yes, but it seems they're all living happily together.'

'You must be one of the best landlords in Ireland, William, but your problem is you care too much. This attitude will never pay our taxes!'

'To hell with our taxes, Maud. I would gladly be forced to leave this big, empty house.' He sank down in the big leather chair and sighed. Maud left to get ready for dinner.

Chapter 8

Mary put another log on the fire. Even though it was October, the house needed a fire during the day to cook and keep the chill away. She poked the embers with an iron poker and just stared at the red yellow flames. Martha came over to her and sat on her knee, putting her arms around her.

'Are you sad, Mary? Do you want to go outside to play?'

'Not today, Martha,' Mary answered kindly. 'Maybe tomorrow, darling.'

Rose came over to the two of them and softly said, 'There's no point in sitting worrying, Mary. It's not going to help bring him back.'

'I really didn't think he would ever do this, Rose. He would never go anywhere without me,' Mary sad sadly.

Rose gently lifted Martha off Mary's knee. 'Go and feed the chickens, my love. That's a girl.'

'He'll come back, Mary. Don't be worrying,' Rose said gently, wiping Mary's tears.

'I know, Ma, but I love him so much. I'm afraid he'll meet someone in his new place and forget about us here - or even forget about me. We talked so much about a new life, a better life away from here, and now that it's happened I just can't believe it,' she said tearfully.

'Mary,' Rose said taking her in her arms. 'God works in ways that we don't understand sometimes, but it is always for our best. If Thomas is meant for you, then one day God will bring him home and you will have a great life together, but for now you must just trust and be patient.'

'I know Ma, but it's still hard,' Mary sobbed, 'I love him so much.'

Thomas sat in the corner of the office in Southampton. The building was on a narrow street where there were small shops selling fishing gear. Above him was a small open window, and he could smell the smell of the sea as well as the fish. He longed to be home, and was now wondering what on earth had possessed him to do such a stupid thing as to come to England with a stranger. The problem was that now he would never find his way home.

Outside, Thomas could hear the two men talking with raised voices but couldn't make out what they were saying. By the look on Charles's face his boss was not pleased with Charles bringing an Irish boy back home with him. After twenty minutes, a stern looking man with a moustache came over to him.

'Well, boy, I'm told that you're looking for work, and that you are a clever young chap.' He examined him closely, and then continued. 'It's very much against our laws here to employ a young boy from Ireland without papers, but as you come with the recommendation of my most senior map surveyor, I'm prepared to offer you an apprenticeship. I'll pay you ten shillings a week till you're trained, and then fifteen shillings a week if you turn out to be as good as Charles says you are.'

'Thank you, sir,' Thomas replied, glancing back at Charles's smiling face. 'I'll do my best.'

The two men went back to the far side of the room and continuing talking until Charles came back and told Thomas it was time to take him to where he would be staying.

They walked for what seemed miles down narrow streets with fish shops and pubs. The streets were dirty. They were filled with very rough looking men, some in uniform and some drunk. He was glad when they turned a corner into what seemed to be a nicer part of the town. The houses had small gardens and there were even trees growing in the street.

Finally, they arrived at a white house that reminded Thomas of the houses from back home - only the thatch was missing. They stopped at the red door and Charles rang the bell with a chain. A friendly stout lady answered the door. She had a long red dress with a white apron tied around her waist.

'This is Thomas from Ireland,' said Charles, as he patted Thomas on the back and moved him to the front door. 'He's is great lad, but this is his first time away from home, so I would be very grateful if you would look after him and make him feel at home.'

'Hello, young Thomas. My name's Elizabeth. You're very welcome.'

'I'll call for you first thing in the morning, Thomas. Then after that you'll be on your own.'

Charles turned and walked away, and Elizabeth showed Thomas through the door into a very clean and tidy house with paintings on the wall and flowers by every window. When he saw his room he just stood transfixed. 'Who will I be sharing this with, ma'am?' he asked quietly.

'Just yourself, son. All paid for by the government department,' she replied as she closed the curtains on the big window that overlooked the sea.

'Is that the only bag you brought with you, son?'

'Yes miss.'

'My last tenant left a lot of clothes behind. I'll see if any of his things might fit you. In the meantime, get a wash in the bathroom next door and come down for a cup of tea.'

When she closed the door Thomas just stood and looked around the room. The walls were painted white and the wooden floor painted black. The furniture was all matching mahogany and the seat in the corner was so soft he didn't want to get up from it.

He walked slowly to the bathroom and was aware of the floor creaking as he went. He had never seen a bathroom before and had no idea what all the contraptions were. There was a basin with two steel taps on it and as he tried one of them and water came pouring out all over him and the floor. He quickly turned it off and realised this was going to be difficult explaining to the lady that he had never been in a bathroom before. The bath back home was a large basin and the hot water came from buckets of hot water which had been heated over the open fire.

Sir William kept his word and sent several telegrams the next day, both to people he knew in Southampton and to the local police. He was surprised when he got a reply from the local police that they would consider the situation for him, but, due to a heavy work load, it may take some time.

He had landed a bombshell on Maud that morning by declaring that he would have to sell a large section of the estate to pay for the taxes that the government were demanding. He told her that he would rather do that than ever put another tenant out of their home. Maud never flinched, as she had never intended to settle in Donegal.

Thomas was in the office going through yet another training session on how to become a map surveyor for the ordnance survey company which now employed him. The man had a black board and was going over figures that Thomas had already learned, and he was now getting slightly bored. Just then there was a knock on the door, and two men came in, along with the manager from downstairs.

'This is Thomas,' the manager said, showing the two men into the room. One of the men was dressed in a policeman's uniform, sporting a strange pointed hat.

'Thomas Sweeney,' said the policeman in a very formal voice which scared Thomas. 'I've reason to believe that you may have been brought here against your will, and it's my job to see that you are returned back to your home.'

The other man moved over beside him and asked rather abruptly, 'What is your real age, young Sweeney?'

'Twenty-one, sir,' lied Thomas, now feeling sick.

'We happen to know your real age, boy. You are only eighteen. Do you know it's illegal to run away before you are twenty-one without consent from your parents?'

'My mother saw me off, sir, and was happy to see me going to England,'

Just then Charles burst into the room behind them. 'Gentlemen,' he began, out of breath. 'What seems to be the problem here?'

'This boy has been kidnapped and brought here against his will, and we are here to make sure he is returned to his parents.'

'It's my fault, gentlemen' announced Charles, 'He worked for me in Ireland and I offered him a job here in England to keep his family from poverty.'

The policeman then turned to Charles. 'And did you know he is only eighteen and has left without his parents' consent?'

'No, sir. He told me he was twenty-one and I certainly didn't force him to come. In fact, I tried to persuade him to go home! His mother and sister are aware of him leaving.'

'We have received a request from Sir William Campbell that he be brought home to his family. They are very worried about him.' All fear suddenly left Thomas as he heard that dreaded name.

'Sir William Campbell? He's no friend of ours!' he gasped. 'He put my family out of our home and burnt the roof!' Just then, however, curiosity gripped him. 'Why on earth would he be looking for me?' The policeman and the man in the suit turned away and whispered something to each other, then turned back to Thomas.

'Did you come here to England by your own free will or were you forced by this gentleman?' asked the policeman.

'I came with Charles because he gave me my first job and promised me a job here in England, which he has done. I've a real chance to make a lot of money now which I can send to my family at home to help them. My father was drowned at sea.' The two men whispered again and called Charles over to them and said something that Thomas couldn't hear.

'Right,' said the policeman. 'It appears that no crime has been committed here and that you are being well looked after. I will allow you to stay - on one condition: That your boss allows you to get a message home to your mother and let her know when you might return.' With that they turned and said goodbye to the manager and walked out the door.

'I'll sort this out,' Charles said to his manager.

'You had better,' was the stern reply. 'Look at the mess you've got me into now. I knew this was a bad idea.'

'He's doing very well, sir, and has progressed much faster than any young trainee we have ever had.'

The manager grunted. 'Eighteen,' he muttered as he left. Charles looked at Thomas with disappointment. 'You nearly got me jailed.'

'I'm really sorry, Charles. I knew you would never take me if I told you my real age, and I needed this so much.'

Charles went over to him and grabbed him by the shoulders. 'One thing, Thomas,' he said sternly. 'You will never ever lie to me again. Is that clear? With lying there's no trust, and with no trust there is no friendship - or job.' He saw the tears in Thomas' eyes, so he put his arm around his shoulder.

'Come with me, lad. You've had enough for one day.'

Chapter 9

3 years later 1845

Thomas and another colleague were down at one of the new harbours under construction on the Southampton sea front. The main construction had been completed in 1843, but a new pier was being built to accommodate the new gigantic ships that were being built in Belfast. Thomas was checking that the construction team were staying within the plans, which were based on the new ordnance survey map.

The clamour, combined with the noise of cranes and trains competing with steam hammers, meant that Thomas didn't hear Charles calling to him from the carriage from which he had just alighted. 'Well, lad,' Charles puffed as he reached Thomas, 'You've done it!' Thomas just stared at him and wondered what was coming next. 'You passed, Thomas! Congratulations!' he said, shaking his hand. 'You're now a fully qualified map surveyor, and your wages go up to fifteen shillings per week.'

Thomas was shocked. Little did he realise that all the tests they had been giving him were part of an examination. He immediately thought of his family at home and how they would react when he tells them. They would be so proud of him!

'There's more good news, Thomas. The boss has said that, because you've done so well, he's going to let you go home for a few weeks; especially since you've been here now for more than three years.' He patted Thomas, who was now smiling from ear to ear. His colleague, Richard, also came over and shook his hand, congratulating him warmly.

'We've just finished here, Charles.' Thomas said, gathering up his equipment. 'The engineers have kept to the measurements on our map from last year, apart from over there where they have gone over the boundary by a few yards, but I presume that since it's all owned by the same company, no one will object.'

'Good man, Thomas. Let me give you two a lift back to the office in my coach. It's far too noisy here to stay any longer.' With that the three of them walked back to the carriage and headed away from the harbour.

'I wouldn't be able to find my way home, Charles. It seemed such a long and complicated journey to get here.'

'Never mind that, son,' Charles replied, laughing. 'I'll book it all for you and give you a map and instructions.'

Thomas was very quiet walking home from the office. He could hardly take in what just happened. Promoted and sent home all in one day! This was hard to believe. How was he going to finish the week's work with the thought of seeing Mary and the family again? Charles kept his word about booking his trip home and presented Thomas with his train and boat tickets, as well as enough money for the coaches and food. The Ordnance survey company was so impressed with Thomas that they had big plans for his future. They decided that they would tell him when he returned from Ireland.

The journey home the following week seemed to go faster than his first journey. He looked so handsome in his smart new clothes that people seemed to go out of their way to make sure he was comfortable. When the final coach stopped in Moville, the spring sun was starting to go down and the air felt a lot cooler than he was used to in Southampton. He took a deep breath of the fresh Donegal air, grabbed his small bag and started the long walk over the mountain to Kinnego.

Thomas passed many small farms and was surprised to see the crops of potatoes all rotting in the ground; the green leaves had all turned brown. 'Seems very quiet about here,' he said to himself as he quickened his pace to get home before it got dark. As he approached his own house he passed his mother's field of potatoes on the left, but the stench turned his stomach.

Bridget was taking some clothes off the outside line at the far end of the house when she heard a voice calling her. At first, she thought she was dreaming. She turned to see someone running up the lane towards the house.

'Ma it's me, I'm home!' he shouted. Bridget dropped the clothes basket and ran to the gate.

'Thomas, my son, she cried, 'and look at you; all grown up and fancy!' They hugged each other, and Thomas lifted her off the ground. He wiped the tears from her eyes and studied closely her tired looking face.

'Is everything all right, ma? You look tired.'

'Not so good right now, son. Have you heard about the potato blight?'

'No, ma. What's that?' he asked, shocked to see his mother so worried.

'The whole potato crop of Ireland has failed, son. Thousands of people are dying of hunger and disease here now.'

'I smelt the rotten crop as I passed, Ma, but what do you mean "The whole of Ireland"?'

'The blight has spared no one, son. Every potato in the land is diseased, and those who have no other food can't afford to buy other crops or meat. It's terrible, son. Terrible!'

'So how you are managing, Ma? Are you, all right?'

'Just about, Thomas, just because Rose and I have always planted other crops and kept a few animals, but now we're having to feed the neighbours to keep them alive. We miss the fish we used to get from your dad and Fergal.'

'Do you get the money I send every month, Ma?'

'We do, son. It's that that's keeping us alive.'

Thomas took his mother by the arm and walked towards the house 'I've been promoted, ma, and with the money I earn now you'll never have to worry again.' As they came to the door Rose came out with Martha.

'Just look who's home, Rose!' Bridget said, with glee.

'Well, thank the good Lord,' shouted Rose, giving Thomas a big hug. 'We were wondering if we'd ever see you again.'

'Ah sure, Rose' Thomas replied, laughing. 'Did I not say I would come back and marry your daughter?'

Rose pulled way and dropped her head. There was an awkward silence for a moment, before Thomas made her look at him. 'What's wrong, Rose? What's wrong?' Thomas dreaded her reply. 'Is she already married?' 'Has something bad happened to her?'

Rose looked at him with tears in her eyes. 'Thomas. I'm sorry. She's gone to America.'

'What!' he said, shocked. 'When?' 'How could she do that?' He was getting angry.

'She thought you might not come back and she was worried about how we would survive. Someone told her there was good work for a girl in America and she got the boat from Londonderry two years ago.' She dropped her head again. 'We haven't heard from her since.'

Everyone was crying now, which upset Martha, who went around hugging each person.

Thomas just turned and stared out at the sunset. He was beginning to wish he hadn't come home.

Bridget took his arm. 'It's getting cold, son. Come in for some dinner.' They all went inside, but he was too annoyed to eat.

Thomas went to work on the farm early the next day. He had seen so many things that need the attention of a man that had not been done since he went away. The first and worst job that he took on was to dig up the rotting potatoes and put them in a pit. It felt good to be back in his old working clothes and, despite the stench, he was still able to enjoy the fresh Donegal air.

'Don't kill yourself,' shouted Bridget from over the wall while she watched her grown up son digging like there was to be no tomorrow. 'Do you need a hand, son?'

'No, Ma. I'm all right. It's just the smell is hard to bear. How long have these been lying here?'

'Only two weeks, Thomas. It just came overnight.'

Thomas stopped digging and went over to his mother. 'Why did I not hear of this in England?'

'The English don't want to know, Thomas. We're on our own here,' Bridget replied, tiredly.

'I don't believe that, Ma. I've found the English to be very kind and generous people and I'm sure if they knew that people were dying of hunger here they would do something about it.'

Bridget could see that Thomas was already being changed in his outlook. After all he'd lived in England for three years. She knew there was no point in telling him about the hundreds of thousands who had already died and what it was going to mean for her community.

Thomas went back to his back-breaking work. 'She should have told me!' He shouted out angrily, 'She had no right to go and leave you all without telling me!' He paused and spat on his hands. 'So much for her faith in a God who, she said, would provide for his people.'

'Never say that again, Thomas,' replied Bridget, raising her voice slightly. 'Rose and Mary's faith has provided for me and you, and don't ever forget it. Thomas had not heard his Mother raise her voice before, and knew he had to change track.

'I was going to come home next year and ask her to marry me,'

'She'll come back, son. Just be patient. She was only thinking of us.' Rose appeared with Martha, and the conversation finished.

At sunset Thomas walked over to Kinnego Bay where his father had drowned. He sat down in his favourite spot where he and Mary would watch the sea. Suddenly everything came back to him, and he sat for a long time just thinking about his present life. What was it all about? He was now earning great money, living in his own small cottage outside Southampton. He was fed and dressed well, had good company in the evening at the local pub and yet coming back here and finding his family in dire straits suddenly made him feel his life was empty. His thoughts were broken by the voice of a man behind him.

'Thinking of going fishing, young Thomas?' the stranger asked.

Thomas turned to see an old friend of his father and Fergal who helped carry him home when they found him on the beach.

'No Sean, I'll never go to sea again.' He smiled at the old man and moved over so he could sit down beside him.

'Why don't you take to the sea again Sean?' asked Thomas, with genuine sadness.

'I have no boat, son. Your da and Fergal had the only boat in these parts. The only place I would find one now is in Greencastle, and they're all owned by the fisherman there.' Thomas looked at the sad face of the old man. 'Have you enough food to live on Sean?'

'I get by, son, but there are many people dying further down the country. Donegal hasn't been as bad so far, thanks be to God.'

'What's this disease that has destroyed the potatoes?' Thomas asked, standing up.

'I don't rightly know, lad. It's like a virus that was blown in with the wind. I looked at my crop growing one night, and they were healthy and when I woke up the next day the leaves were all brown. A few days later, the potatoes were all rotten.'

Sean stood up and made to go. 'I've got a few shillings,' said Thomas, awkwardly reaching into his pocket. 'My da would want me to give them to you.' Sean was about to refuse but knew it might keep him alive a few more months.

'Like father, like son,' he said, as he accepted the money. 'One day I'll repay you for your kindness.'

'There's no need, my friend. Be careful how you spend it. Maybe buy some new seed potato for next spring.' Sean shook his hand and turned and walked away. Thomas went home.

Over the next ten days Thomas worked frantically as he tried to get his farm into shape. It was too early and wet to cut the turf, but he did it anyway. He fixed fences and the chicken run and cut up logs for next winter's fire. All he could think off was Mary and what might have happened to her. He promised himself that one day he would go to America to find her.

It was a cold wet Irish morning when it was time to say goodbye once again, and the only good thing in his mind was that he now had renewed purpose to do well in his job so that one day he could return to look after his family. Bridget, Rose and Martha stood by the door as he pulled his big coat up round his shoulders and lifted his travelling bag.

'Expect a lot of money next month and buy yourselves some good food in Moville,' he said, with tears in his eyes. 'I'll be back home again soon.' He paused, looking out to sea. 'If you hear from Mary, let me know right away, now.' He wouldn't wait for a reply as he knew it would be too hard to say any more, so with that he turned and walked down the lane.

Chapter 10

Maud was finishing her breakfast when Sir William came in with a newspaper. 'This isn't good Maud, not good at all.' He dropped the paper down on the table in front of her. 'What are we going to do?'

Maud looked at the front page of the paper and continued eating her toast and tea. 'Why do you think there is anything that we can do, William, when our own government does nothing?'

Sir William sat down at the other end of the long dining room table and began eating his breakfast.

'Fancy us just sitting here having a nice breakfast and a big dinner tonight while half the country is starving! We need to do something.'

'What can we do, William, when we're nearly bankrupt ourselves?'

'Yes, but we eat - and eat well - while a few miles from here people are dying because they haven't eaten for months.'

'The people brought it on themselves,' she replied. 'How stupid to rely on only one crop to live.'

Sir William slammed his fist on the table. 'That is the worst thing I've ever heard you say Maud! An absolute disgrace! They only have potatoes because they can only afford potatoes and now they have no potatoes. What would you have them do?' Maud knew Sir William was at exploding point and was quite capable of making rash decisions when he was like that, so she tried to be more conciliatory.

'How do you think we can help them, William?

William was quiet as he sat and looked out the window. He got up from his seat with a piece of toast in his hand. 'I shall start a collection and then I will contact London to see why they're not shipping grain and food to Dublin,' he said, resolutely.

'Do you expect the poor to give you money to feed the poor?' Maud asked, cynically.

'No Maud.' He turned to face her. 'I'm going to start a collection from our aristocratic friends who, for once, will give back to this land what we have taken from it.'

'Be very careful, William. You could end up having no friends. We might need them in years to come.' William walked out of the room, determined to call the estate manager.

Thomas was early for his first day back in the office, and was surprised to see his senior boss already at his desk. He was about to sit down at his table when his boss waved at him to come into his office. 'Oh dear,' thought Thomas. 'I wonder what I have done wrong.' Sydney his boss invited him to take seat while he lifted a large map from a table at the right side of the office.

'Good to see you, Thomas. Come in and take a seat while I unfold this chart. Did you've a good time back home, lad?'

'Yes, thank you, sir,' replied Thomas, although he was tempted to mention the potato blight.

'This estate belongs to Lord Shrewsbury, Thomas. It's is over 6000 acres of valuable land.'

He placed the very old map in front of Thomas. 'The only problem is that this map is long out of date and so has little value to the owner. Now we have been asked by the crown to do a new survey of the estate. The government has some vested interest in the land that we are not being told about.'

Sydney sat down opposite Thomas and threw the map on the floor. 'Now, young man, I believe the time has come, since your promotion, to appoint you to your new assignment, and I am going to trust you as senior surveyor to oversee this project.' Thomas was shocked and didn't know what to say.

He continued, 'The lord has agreed to let you move into one of his cottages on the estate where you and whoever you chose to go with you shall stay for the year that it will take to survey the six thousand acres. You will have full access to every part of the estate and will be looked after by the lord's staff who will provide you with everything you request. If you succeed in doing a good job on this, Thomas, there will be more promotion for you at the end.' Thomas sat completely dumbstruck. 'I know it is a big task young man, but one I have full confidence in you to achieve. Will you do it?'

'Of course, sir' Thomas stuttered. 'I'm just shocked that you've chosen me above others in the company who would be more skilled than I.'

'More skilled is right, Thomas, but no other employee invents new ways of doing things as they go along like you do. You've already invented new practices that are now being used in other places.'

Sydney got up from his seat and shook Thomas's hand. 'Well done, son. I knew you would do it! Now go and pack your things and get ready for the train journey tomorrow, and - oh yes - who would you like to work with you?'

'I'll have a think about that, sir,' replied Thomas, in a daze.

'Good, lad. You have only ten minutes as I'll need to tell the other person to get ready as well.' Thomas walked out of the office wondering if he was dreaming. 'How could this be happening to him, a young lad from Donegal!'

The only person that he could think to accompany him was Richard.

Richard was a hard worker, but also good fun, and the two of them had become close friends as they worked together every day on their maps. Thomas met Richard at the railway station and the two of them couldn't stop talking with excitement. Thomas was excited as this was his first major project as a senior map surveyor, and Richard, as he was looking forward to getting out to the country for a year.

'This is the life Thomas,' said Richard, as he looked around their first-class compartment 'Thank you so much for asking for me.'

'Hmm. Just don't let me down, Richard. By right I should have taken one of the older men, but I thought you were looking a bit pale and needed some country air.' Thomas threw his case onto the rack above the seat and then opened the window as the train started to pull out. 'This is a very big project. Richard. It'll be hours of hard work.' He paused, and then smiled at Richard. 'But it'll also be hours of fun for us.'

The black smoke from the steam engine blocked out the view of the dirty old houses that seemed to go and on, until at last green fields appeared. It was a long journey and the two young men had fallen asleep when a guard knocked on their door to tell them they had arrived at their destination.

It was getting dark as they made their way out of the tiny country station, but as the train pulled out they could both now smell the country air. 'Gentlemen,' said a man in a black suit, as he approached them from the road. 'Would you be masters Thomas and Richard, by any chance?'

'Yes, we are,' replied Thomas, about to shake his hand. The man didn't offer his hand in return but replied in a very posh accent, 'I am only the driver, gentlemen. I have come to fetch you. Please follow me.'

Thomas and Richard looked at each other, sniggering, as he turned and walked towards a black shining carriage with four majestic horses.

'I am to take you, his lordship, on to your cottage. I believe he has organised a supper for you both.' Thomas and Richard climbed into the carriage while the driver put their bags into a luggage box at the back. 'Twenty minute drive,' were the last words they heard before the driver climbed on the front seat.

'This is really posh,' whispered Richard, looking a bit wary. 'I didn't think we were going to meet the lord himself!'

'Relax Richard' replied Thomas, reaching over and patting his knee. 'Just remember they need us right now more than we need them, and we are professionals.'

They could just about see the long driveway that the carriage turned into but could see the lights of the huge estate house at the far end.

'Blimey' said Richard. 'It looks like the king's palace in London!' Thomas didn't reply. He suddenly had a strange knot in his stomach as he cast his mind back to the landlord's estate in Moville, Co. Donegal. The carriage passed the front door and went around to a side entrance where the driver stopped and opened the door for them. 'Ring the bell, gentlemen, and someone will let you in,' the driver said, as he collected their cases.

They had hardly pulled the bell cord when the door opened, and they were invited in by another man in a black suit. He showed them into a large room with a long wooden table where a meal was set out waiting for them. 'Please, gentlemen, help yourselves. His lordship will see you when you are finished.' With that they were alone and sat down to one of the biggest feasts that either of them had ever seen.

They had just finished eating when the large door at the end of the room opened and Lord Shrewsbury came in. He was a small round man with a red smiling face and seemed to almost bounce while he walked. 'Gentlemen, don't get up,' he said, smiling, as he pulled the end seat out and sat down beside them. At the same time, the other door opened, and the butler appeared, flustered. 'I'm sorry, my lord. I was going to bring these folks in to see you.'

'Never mind,' Lord Shrewsbury replied, dismissing the butler and turning to Thomas. 'Now I've been told that you, Mr. Thomas, are one of the best up and coming map surveyors in the country. You have been highly spoken of by your boss, only I'm surprised to see that you are so young.' Thomas was about to reply but wasn't given the opportunity.

'Now then, young man, no doubt you've been made aware of what's happening here. It's my intention to make my estate more workable and earn some money for its keep. I have plans - big plans - plans that many don't like, but that doesn't bother me in the slightest.' He laughed jovially. Thomas could see that he was a genuine, cheery sort of man who looked as if he enjoyed life, but also one who wouldn't take no for an answer. He had him summed him up within five minutes of meeting him. He liked him, and was pretty confident that they'd get on well.

'First, I need to see just how much land I actually own.' He continued pouring himself a glass of wine. 'I need to see how much could possibly be used to extend two of the local villages. This is where you two lads come in, as the whole estate will have to be surveyed properly - particularly at the west end. That's where the government has asked me to sell land for a new road and railway. I told them that if they want any of my estate, then they must pay for a proper survey to be carried out; hence, they have ordered the ordnance survey company to do it.

I know that you don't normally do this type of private work, but then our present government isn't that ordinary either.' He gave another big laugh.

He stood up and looked at Thomas. 'Now then, Mr. Thomas. I am giving you full access to my estate from this moment on. You shall have the full support of all my staff, and all my carriages and horses are at your disposal. You will also have access to all these grounds. The house manager will show you to your cottage, which is only half a mile away. All your food will be supplied, and a cleaner will come in once a week.

I have two children, Edward and Christina. who are about your age. You'll see them come and go from time to time. My son does not approve of my new plans, but he has been well warned not to interfere with that.' He rang a bell and the butler appeared. 'Ask Byron to take my two friends to the cottage and make arrangements for them for the morning.' Lord Shrewsbury then turned and opened the door and, looking back. 'Welcome to my world, gentlemen. I hope you'll enjoy your stay here. Let me know what you need.'

The lights were on the cottage as they arrived, and Thomas could smell the wood fire smoke from outside the quaint house. The cottage was bigger than any house he had seen in Ireland.

He turned to the driver as they were being shown in and asked, 'How many other people will be sharing the house with us?'

'Just you for you gentlemen,' the driver replied, curtly. 'What time would you like me to be here in the morning, sir?'

'It won't be necessary tomorrow as we're better just walking about for our first few days.'

Chapter 11

The next four months were hard work. Thomas had only old maps that were out of date. It was difficult to see where the estate was supposed to begin and end, and he found it more useful to ask labourers and neighbours. In the end Thomas decided that the best way for them to get their bearings was to start with the main house and work from there. They now had a rough idea of the boundary, so it was time to start making draft maps.

Summer came early in the West Country that year and the two lads enjoyed working in the warm sunshine. They were measuring a piece of garden that went down to a huge lake hidden in the trees when suddenly Richard grabbed Thomas by the arm. 'Who's that, Thomas?' he gasped, pointing. The two were very quiet for a moment as they just stood and gazed at a young girl stroking a horse as it drank from the side of the lake.

The girl looked up suddenly and saw them staring at her and then watched them nervously out of the corner of her eye. Finally, she walked boldly over to them. 'Who are you, gentlemen, and why are you on my land?' She asked, pulling the horse round so that they could see this was a stallion of rare breeding and looked like something out of an old masterpiece.

'We're surveyors, miss. Lord Shrewsbury hired us to make maps of his land.

'Oh. Forgive me, gentlemen. My father did tell me before Christmas that you would be working here. It's just that I expected two old men, not two handsome young men - and so well turned out,' she smiled.

Thomas and Richard had never met any girl so full of self confidence, but they had also never seen a more beautiful girl! Thomas was transfixed. She had the loveliest sparkling blue eyes and long golden hair flowing down her slim back and waist. Richard, realising that Thomas was just standing staring at the girl, nudged him. 'Your father never told us that he had such a beautiful daughter, miss. We're very glad to make your acquaintance.' Richard ventured. However, he noticed that the girl was also looking at Thomas intently.

'My name is Christina, and my father likes to hide me away from young men.' She smiled. 'He wants to train me to take over this land one day with my brother and he thinks it better that I do that without the influence of men.'

'Begging your pardon, miss,' replied Thomas, now feeling embarrassed. 'My apologies. It's just taken us by surprise to meet you here in the woods.'

'Yes, miss,' stuttered Richard. 'We spend our lives measuring things, meeting very few folks out in the open countryside, so it is very nice to meet people now and again.' They both knew that they were out of their depth as Christina chuckled like her father and turned her horse to walk away. 'I'm going to enjoy meeting you two gentlemen again, soon, I hope.' With that she was gone.

Thomas stared after her as she disappeared through the trees, before picking up his instruments. 'I've never seen you stuck for words before, Thomas,' Richard joked. patting him on the back. Thomas shook his head and went back to work.

It was such a warm pleasant evening that Thomas and Richard ate their dinners outside with the plates set on their knees. Richard was chatting away about what they done for the day, but Thomas was eating slowly and was unusually quiet. Richard turned to Thomas and stole the end of his beer 'Don't even think about it, Thomas,' he said. gulping the beer back. Thomas looked at Richard. 'I've fallen in love with someone I don't even know, Richard. It's such a strange feeling.' Then added under his breath, 'She's different from Mary.'

'Who's Mary?' asked Richard, surprised

'We grew up together in Ireland.'

'Oh dear. This isn't good. You only saw this girl for five minutes. How could you be in love with someone in that time? She's the lord's daughter, for goodness' sakes. Now do you think for one minute that the lord's daughter would be remotely interested in a working-class man like you?'

'Yes,' replied Thomas. 'I know she feels the same.'

Richard spat the last of the beer on the ground and jumped up. 'Oh, come on, Thomas. She was just surprised to see us. What makes you think she likes you?'

'I saw it in her eyes, Richard. Our hearts met in her eyes.'

'Ah! You've got it bad, Thomas. You'll be ok tomorrow. I'm off to bed.'

Thomas got up, laughing. 'I know, but a man has to dream, doesn't he? Now, where's my beer gone?' When Thomas found that Richard had finished it all he chased him into the house.

By the end of April, the map was already taking shape and Thomas was surprised at how easy the work turned out to be. It was hard to believe that they were getting paid to spend so much time in the warm sunshine surrounded by the beautiful English countryside. They requested a coach for the day as Thomas wanted to measure a huge valley at the east side of the estate.

As the coach pulled up at the door of the cottage. they were surprised to find Lord Shrewsbury was waiting in the back for them. 'Now, boys,' he chortled, I'm coming with you today as I want to see what you make of my valley.' Thomas and Richard climbed up into the carriage and immediately the driver took off. 'You met my Christina,' Lord Shrewsbury enquired suddenly, looking at Thomas. He could see the uneasiness in Thomas's face and immediately gave another hearty laugh. 'It's quite all right, son. You appear to have made quite an impression on her.'

Now Thomas was sure he was about to be sent home. Lord Shrewsbury looked out the window. 'Some day I shall leave her half of this, and she'll need a good man to take care of her. Because of her title there are few good men as most come after her for her money, you know, Thomas.' Thomas had no idea how to reply to this statement, so he just smiled and looked nervously at Richard.

'Where did you say you were from, son?'

'County Donegal in Ireland, sir.'

'I see,' said Lord Shrewsbury. 'And what line of business is your family in Thomas?'

'My father owned a fishing business,' Thomas lied 'until he drowned at sea three years ago.'

'I'm sorry to hear that young man.'

An hour later the coach stopped by an old stone bridge with a stream running under it. The view over the valley was one of the most spectacular in all of England. 'This stream, Thomas,' started the lord, has he jumped out of the coach, 'is the start of what turns into a river at the far end of my estate. A local engineer wants to harness the water for generating electricity. The government has asked me to sell them land at the far end of the valley so that they can create a weir. They then want me to work with this engineer to develop a whole new town on the far end of the weir. The money they would give me would mean my estate would last another one hundred years without me doing one day's work.' He paused and showed Thomas and Richard the boundary line.

'This is the most important part of your work, as a lot depends on an accurate map of this valley.'

'This will take a few days to measure this properly, my lord, but it should be fairly straightforward.'

'Good, lads. If you get this part done, by the end of the week I'll invite you both to a party I am having on Saturday at my house.'

Thomas and Richard were exhausted by Friday evening as they were determined to get the valley finished. Nevertheless, Thomas really wanted to go to the house to see Christina again. As they were cleaning up after dinner on Friday evening the house butler came to the door and invited them to come to the house at seven pm sharp and ensure sure that they were suitably dressed for the party. Richard could hardly get Thomas to stop talking as he was trying to get to sleep, but Thomas couldn't stop thinking the party - mostly about meeting Christina again.

Chapter 12

Thomas and Richard walked the short distance from the cottage to the main house and were amazed at the number of very expensive looking carriages that passed them on the way up the drive way. 'How on earth will we fit in here tonight?' asked Richard, smoothing his hair.

'We won't,' laughed Thomas.

'Well you won't anyway.'

'We'll find a quiet spot to hide, and eat as much food and drink as much wine as we can. Then we'll fill our pockets.'

'On a soberer note about food, Thomas, I was talking today to man in the village who told me that there are thousands of your folks dying in Ireland right now because they have no food. Is that correct?'

Thomas stopped as if he had been hit by lightning.

'What did you hear Richard? Which part of Ireland' he asked, with great panic in his voice.

'The man said that the potato crop had failed over all the land and many people were starving to death.'

'I know about the potato blight, Richard,' said Thomas looking at the ground. 'It was just starting when I went home last, but I thought it would only be for a short time.'

Richard was sorry that he brought this up now as they were about to eat a lot of food. Thomas turned and walked on towards the house. 'I plan to go home again when we're finished here, Richard, but tonight I must try and put it out of my mind.' They didn't feel right walking in the front door, so they went around to the side door that they used when they first came to the house. They were about to go inside when a voice stopped them.

'Now where would you two gentlemen be going?' They both turned and there was Christina watching them. She was wearing a light blue chiffon dress, which perfectly matched her clear blue eyes and complimented her golden blond locks which fell loosely around her delicate shoulders. She looked an absolute picture, and the two lads were speechless!

'How nice to meet you again. Come this way, gentlemen.' She brought them back to the front door. 'You are just as important as any of my father's boring friends that are here tonight, and so long as you stick with me, you shall be just fine.'

The front reception area was huge! The glass chandeliers sparkled against the ornate, painted ceiling. 'How on earth did some poor soul paint those from down here?' Richard asked, laughing. 'He must have had wings.' Thomas just stared at the wealth that he never knew existed.

'The wealth in here would feed everyone who's presently dying in my country, Richard,' Thomas said, with a sigh.

'What are your names?' asked Christina, moving into the midst of all the finely dressed people surrounding her father.

'I'm Richard, and this is Thomas. He's from Ireland'

'From Ireland? Oh! I didn't know that - I mean - not that that matters. I just couldn't place your accent, that's all.' Thomas met her eyes again and felt a burning in his chest. He looked away.

'Father, I brought Thomas and Richard, as you requested,' Christina announced as she moved beside him. The crowd parted to let the two lads into the middle of the circle.

'Ladies and gentlemen,' announced Lord Shrewsbury. 'May I have your attention please!' He walked over beside the lads and put a hand on each shoulder. 'I would like to introduce you to my new friends from the ordnance survey company who are here, at my request, to help me become even richer than I am now.' He gave a big laugh, and everyone responded. 'They're the finest government employees in the country, so please make them at home.' With that he got the waiter to give them a glass of wine each and then turned back to his friends. Christina rescued them and put her arm under Thomas's arm and let them to quiet corner.

Two very well dressed young men were standing by the huge staircase drinking large amounts of alcohol. One was twenty and tall, the other twenty-five, short and stout.

'My father is a complete fool, Malcolm,' said the tall one. He turned and sneered at his father. 'He thinks he can sell off my inheritance before he departs and leaves me with a pension and a hovel.'

I'm sure he'll leave you most of this. Edward' replied Malcolm, now talking with slurred speech. 'Most of the land isn't used anyway.'

'Be quiet, Malcolm,' Edward replied, angrily. 'I can farm this land as my grandfather did and restore it to its glory again, and we shall have banquets far greater than this. We shall invite the most beautiful women in the world to join us here.'

'What would do with them all?' he laughed.

'You wouldn't know, you fool.' Edward sneered, and took another glass of wine. Then, nodding his head towards Thomas and Richard, 'I don't want these two gold-diggers on my land. We need to get rid of them.'

Christina pointed at the two men and said with a wistful sigh. 'That's my brother, Edward, over there beside the small, stout man. He doesn't get on well with Father. He didn't turn out the way my father imagined, and once my mother died, my father became very strict with him. They don't see eye to eye at all.'

'I couldn't imagine your father being anything but generous and polite,' Thomas said, surprised. 'I'm very sorry to hear about your mother. Is it a long time since she passed away?' Thomas asked, awkwardly. She didn't answer as there was an announcement from the butler that dinner was served, and all the guests started to file into the grand dining room at the right end of the hall.

'I was thinking, Thomas, that perhaps after dinner you would like to escort me for a walk in our flower garden at the back. I could show you our new fountains.' Thomas was shocked, but quickly agreed, with a quip, 'Would you feel safe walking with an Irishman?' Christina looked at him for about twenty seconds and knew she was falling in love with the most wonderful man she had ever met. 'Should I feel otherwise?' she laughed.

'It would be my pleasure. Christina, but first you need to help us common men get through this dinner.'

'What are all these knives and forks for,' asked Richard.

'Just follow me, gentlemen, and you'll be fine - and don't let anyone try and put you down.'

'I can't believe that anyone could eat that much food in one meal,' said Richard, patting his stomach, 'but it feels jolly good! May we come again, Christina?'

'Believe me, Richard, you would soon bore of this company and food as I have. I long to live a life as free as you two men do.' Thomas looked at Christina again and could see a sadness in her eyes for the first time, realising that there was a lot more to this beautiful woman than just her looks.

Thomas asked Richard to go and talk to Edward and see if they could meet for a chat next week. It was a good rouse, and as soon as Richard walked across the room, Christina turned to Thomas. pointing towards the arched door. 'The garden, then, young man.' Christina took his hand as they walked out a huge glass door which led straight into a magnificent rose garden with three majestic fountains, all with different themes.

'This is amazing!' gasped Thomas. 'Some amount of thought and clever design gone into this project.'

'Thank you, Thomas. It's the one thing that father has allowed me do.' She wouldn't let go of his hand. and Thomas thought he could feel her very heart beat through his arm. He had never had this feeling before. Mary had been like a sister to him growing up, and he loved her. When she kissed him, it was very nice, but didn't seem right. He had never had feelings for any girl but Mary, but now this was almost uncontrollable. They reached the edge of the fountain, designed in the shape of a large white stallion. The water poured out of its mouth down onto a green base that was like grass.

Christina sat down on the side of the pond and motioned for Thomas do the same. 'I know this seems ludicrous, Thomas, but all my life I've dreamed of a life outside of this charade. I am grateful for all I have got, but the trouble, is I have everything and yet nothing.' She paused, and let go of his hand to throw a pebble into the pond. 'My father has introduced me to many handsome young men in the hope that I would marry into money and position. I'm tired of their pretense. All they ever desire are two things - my looks and my money.'

'That's a big part of this life, Christina. I'm sure it can't be all bad,' Thomas tried to reassure her. 'I'm sure there must be some very genuine, good men out there. In fact, I've met quite a few in my work.'

'If I could blindfold them first, Thomas, so they wouldn't know what I look like but who I really am, then maybe I would find someone.'

Thomas moved closer to her and said softly. 'Any man who couldn't fall in love with you, Christina, would be a fool.'

She looked at him gently again and held both his hands. 'This has never happened to me before. We know nothing of each other, but I fell in love with you the moment you stepped out from behind the tree at the lake. I knew by your eyes that you are a man who knows what real life is, and I could tell that you are a man of deep understanding. It was as if I were looking into the eyes of someone who could love deeply.'

Thomas was quiet for a while and then said, sadly, 'I come from a very poor family in Ireland, Christina; living in a very poor part of a poor country, and all this is like a dream to me.' Then he studied her beautiful face. 'But right now, in the middle of this dream is where I want to remain.'

'When I look into your eyes, Thomas, it's as if I see my own soul. It's so strange. I've never met any human being whose eyes seem to know what I am thinking.' Christina said, wistfully.

'If you knew right now, Christina, what I am thinking, there would be no need to have this conversation at all,' Thomas laughed, gently.

After a short pause, Christina lent forward and kissed Thomas on the lips. His whole body shook, and he felt like he was on his boat again at Kinnego bay with the blue sea and crashing waves. They parted for a few seconds, then kissed passionately again. After a few seconds, they could hear Richard's voice calling for them.

'What do we do now Christina?' whispered Thomas. Just then Richard appeared from around the nearest fountain.

'I don't know, Thomas. I'll contact you some way,' Christiana whispered, urgently.

Thomas couldn't sleep, so he got out of his bed and went and sat by the dying fire in his living room. He picked up a half-finished bottle of beer and sat down on the wicker seat, his legs outstretched before him. Richard suddenly appeared and sat down opposite him.

'You're not sleeping either, I see,' he grunted. 'That was a night to remember!'

'It certainly was, Richard. It certainly was.' he smiled.

'The lord's son doesn't like us and made that very clear when you sent me to talk to him. I was very close to giving him a clout'.

'I'm very glad you didn't, Richard! You would have been just slightly outnumbered.'

Richard puffed at his pipe and took some of the bottle that Thomas had been drinking.

'I don't know what to do now, Richard.' Thomas said, turning one of the logs on the fire. 'I'm in very big trouble.'

'What sort of trouble, Thomas?' Richard sat up, alarmed.

'Christina kissed me.' Richard spat the drink out into the fire in shock.

'What!' he exhaled. There was silence between them as Richard could see that Thomas was not joking. 'You've more than trouble, Thomas. You're in deep water, now, my friend.' After some thought, Richard stood up. 'Are ye soft in the head?' Richard now railed 'What on earth makes you think for one minute that the lord's daughter would be even remotely interested in you, really? Why did you let her kiss you? She's only playing with you!'

'I could do nothing Richard. She kissed me.'

Richard jumped up and ran to the cupboard where they kept their drink and opened a bottle of whiskey. 'This can't be happening,' he whimpered. 'This cannot be happening! 'What if the lord finds out? We'll both be finished, and I'll be sent home to Yorkshire in disgrace.'

'Calm down, Richard That's all that happened.'

'That is all? Sweet mercy! Christina, the lord's daughter kissed the surveyor out in his own garden? Oh sure. Nothing happened!' he moaned, sarcastically.

Thomas knew nothing would calm him down. He got up from the chair. 'I'm away to bed now, Richard. You'll be quite fine. Enjoy your night cap.' Richard poured himself a double and swallowed it in one gulp before collapsing into the chair.

That night, Thomas lay in bed staring at the ceiling. 'What have I just done?' he thought. He remembered Mary back home whom he had promised to marry, but now he was beginning to realise that he loved Mary as a friend but not as a girlfriend. This was the first time his heart was pounding like this and he felt something that he never knew existed. He could still feel the passionate embrace of an hour ago. It was the best feeling in the world.

He heard Richard close the door of his bedroom next to his but suddenly fear gripped him again. 'What if the lord finds out about their secret embrace? Would he be dismissed? Would he be shot? Would he lock his daughter away forever, and it would be all his fault?'

Chapter 13

It was raining heavily the next day, so Thomas decided that, since they hadn't had a day off from the time they started, they should walk the mile into the village. Richard grumbled, but eventually gave in, and the two of them set off after lunch. They spent several hours looking at the small shops with their flower boxes adorning the windows and climbing roses around the doors.

It was a quiet Sunday and several coaches were parked in the open square. The rain stopped, and the smell of fresh flowers was mixed with the smell of a roast pig that was being cooked on a spit at the side of the one and only pub. 'That smells good Richard,' Thomas said, patting him on the back, 'but right now you're going to buy me a pint, my dear English friend – although, you know, it's never as good as our Guinness,' he said, teasingly.

There were only a dozen people in the bar, and most were sitting talking at wooden tables. Thomas notice that the two men standing at the far end of the bar counter appeared to be slightly drunk. One of them turned as they came in, and Thomas was surprised to see it was the Edward who he had met last night. He stared at Thomas, and Thomas detected a look of hatred in his eyes. When the drinks were handed to them they went and sat down and the far end of the lounge, as far as possible from Edward. They didn't have to wait long, however, before the two men came and stood in front of them.

'Let me make myself clear, men,' Edward started in a low voice, 'I am set to inherit my father's estate one day - all of it. I am not prepared to watch him try and sell it off to fools and government departments just because he wants to give money to my sister and pay off some of his debts. I intend to make this estate great again without selling one acre of it.'

He paused and came close to Thomas, looking him straight in the face.' I would suggest that you and this ratbag who is with you pack your little bags and leave. if you know what's good for you. Your services are no longer required, and if you don't go it may happen that you will have an accident. We wouldn't want that to happen, would we?'

Thomas just stared back and said nothing, even though he wanted to lunge out at this obnoxious young man. He pinched Richard's hand beside him to make sure he wouldn't react either.

'This will be my one and only warning.' He swayed slightly before the other man took his arm and pulled him away.

Thomas continued his drink, and smiled at Richard. who looked very scared. 'They mean it, Thomas. We need to go.'

'Relax Richard. I'm not afraid of any Englishman; especially not a spoilt brat like that!'

'We need to tell his lordship, Thomas, I don't wish to have an accident.'

'There will be no accident, Richard. Now enjoy the rest of your pint.'

When they got back to the cottage there was a note on the door. Thomas pulled it off and read it out loud to Richard. 'Meet me in the stables at eight. Christina.'

'Awe no, Thomas. This isn't good. One of the lord's children wants to kill you and the other one wants to kiss you! What have you got us into, Thomas?'

'Go and make us a nice brew, Richard, while I figure this out.'

There were carriages coming and going up and down the driveway to the house, so Thomas had to keep ducking in behind trees. The stables were at the far side of the house, and the only way was for Thomas to wait till there was no one about, and then sneak past the front door and windows in hope that no one would see him. The stables were in a long building with a thatched roof and could hold up to twenty horses. There was one oil light hanging from a pole outside the main door.

Thomas moved slowly as he was sure someone would suddenly step out of one of the stalls and find him. Inside, another single light lit the long corridor covered in hay and straw. He stopped and wondered whether he had done the right thing, when suddenly a soft hand came from behind and covered his face. He would have fought it away, only he could smell the same perfume from last night.

'You came,' said Christina, in a soft seductive voice. 'I had to see you again.' She turned Thomas round to face her and kissed him hard on the lips.

'What if someone finds us here Christina?' Thomas gasped between kisses, and pulled away.

'There's yet another boring party in the house. No one will ever come out here at this time.' With that she led Thomas to an empty stall and closed the steel gate behind them. Thomas and Christiana lay on the floor on new straw and kissed passionately. Time seemed to stand still for a little while, until, eventually, they just lay there staring into each other's eyes.

There was a long silence. Then Thomas said hesitantly, 'How can this work? I mean, you're the daughter of nobility. I'm a working man from Ireland. Will this dream come to an end?'

'Leave it to me, Thomas. I'll work on my father.'

'It's not just your father I'm worried about. We met your brother today in the village and he told me that if I didn't leave that I might have an accident as he doesn't want your father to sell off parts of the estate.'

'My brother is a sad person Thomas. He has always only been concerned for himself since my mother died. He doesn't care for me or my father. He wouldn't touch you. He's afraid of me because I think things through, while he just spends time drinking away his inheritance.'

They moved to the front door and Christina told Thomas to be careful going back. With that, she ran across the yard to the back door. Thomas crouched down and walked slowly past the front of the house. What he didn't see that was a man was hiding in a doorway watching them both before he slipped inside as well. Thomas went to bed that night thinking that he had been transported to heaven.

The next morning was Monday, and Christina joined her father for breakfast. He was busy reading a newspaper while she finished her scrambled eggs on toast. She was nervous about what she was about to ask her father, and so drank an extra coffee. 'Father.' She paused to see if he would give her his full attention, but he kept on reading.

'Yes darling?' he replied, eventually, turning the page.

'You once told me that, despite the many times you've introduced me to fine men, you would always let me marry for love and not position.'

Lord Shrewsbury looked over his paper with expectation that what he was about to hear next might not be good. 'Go on,' he said slowly.

'Well, Father. It's just that I've fallen in love with the most amazing man.' There was silence from the lord. He gazed at her intensely. 'The man I love has no title; in fact, he's a working man - a hardworking man at that - but a real honest kind man.'

'I see,' replied the lord. 'And who might this wonderful man be?'

'Hmm, someone who is working for you right now, father: Thomas the surveyor.' There was a long silence again till the lord stood up.

'Christina, please take heed, my dear. I want you to marry for love, darling, but you must choose very carefully. Thomas is from Ireland and we know very little about him apart from the reference he comes with from the ordnance survey company.'

'Yes, but Father, I've never known love until now! I just know in my heart that Thomas isn't just kind, but a he is a true gentleman.' There was a long silence before Lord Shrewsbury took his daughters hands in his own.

'There is so much of your mother in you, my love. She always looked for the best in people.'

'That's why she married you, Daddy,' Christina replied, throwing her arms him.

'Well, my love, if you think Thomas may be the one, let me have a long think about it.'

'Oh, Father, thank you! I love you so much! You're the best father anyone could wish for'

'Now easy my love. I still haven't given my decision yet.'

Christina hugged her father again. 'If Thomas were to ask me to marry him, which he has not yet done yet, what might you say?'

'I told you, Christina. We must know more about this Thomas boy from Ireland. If I were to allow you to marry him, then he would inherit part of my family estate, and I'm not going to give that away too swiftly. I will need some time Christina'

'Oh, thank you, Daddy. I love you so much.'

Christina ran happily out of the room. The world had suddenly become a much brighter place.

Chapter 14

Edward stumbled heavily out of bed and looked out his bedroom window, still suffering the effects of last night's party. He stood watching his father with some distain as he alighted from his coach and came through the front door, then summoned the butler.

'You rang, sir?'

'Yes. Where's my breakfast, and where on earth are the clothes I left out for washing yesterday?'

'Right away, sir. I'll see to both,' he answered, as he left quickly. 'Your friend is downstairs, sir.'

'Send the fool up,' Edward shouted in anger.

Malcolm entered the room as Edward was finishing pulling on his clothes. 'You look some sight, Edward!' he said, picking up some of Edward's clothes and putting them on the bed.

'Leave those! Let my servants do that'. Edward snapped as he splashed water on his face.

He came over to Malcolm, pointing his finger out the window. 'This estate. I don't intend to share it with my sister or anyone else, and I certainly have no intention of letting my father sell any of this to the government!'

'It sounds like he has plans to make a lot of money out of it, Edward. That might be good for you, eventually.' Edward grabbed a bottle of whiskey that a small amount left in it from his drinking last night. He gulped it down in one go and threw the empty bottle onto the fireplace, covering the floor in broken glass.

'Come along, Malcolm. We have some plans to make.' The two of them ran down the four flights of wooden stairs and jumped the last few steps to land together in a heap on the polished floor facing the front door. Just then Lord Shrewsbury came out of the living room door.

'What are you two doing? Are you still drunk Edward?' Edward feared his father and tried to stand up quickly. He didn't even try to answer, as he knew his father wouldn't listen to him. The butler appeared from the kitchen carrying the breakfast tray.

'Take these two drunks out of my sight and try and sober them up,' he shouted to the butler.

'I'll talk to you later.' He pointed his finger at Edward, threateningly, and stormed out of the front door. Edward and Malcolm followed the butler back into the kitchen where they slumped down at the kitchen table.

'Leave us,' he said abruptly to the butler.

'Now, listen well, we have plans to make.' Edward said, as he divided half of his breakfast onto another plate for Malcolm.

'What plans?' asked Malcolm, very nervously.

'I've got to get rid of the two gold-diggers before one of them robs me of my entire inheritance; especially since I saw my sister with the Irish boy last night. If there's a chance that she will inherit half of this place and then share it with that farmer, then she will have to go too.'

'Edward, you can't be serious!'

Sir William was covered in mud and soaked to the skin. 'In here,' he shouted to a man and his wife as he helped them down from a cart. 'Quickly! Get in out of the rain and get warmed up by the fire.' He showed the elderly couple through the door and dropped their bag beside the fire. 'Sit there and I'll tell Maud that you are ready to eat.' The man was quite tall at one time, but hunger and stress had worn him down and now he was badly stooped over. The woman was probably pretty in her youth, but now her face was haggard with pain and worry.

'You'll be all right now, folks,' said Sir William. 'This will be your home until times change.'

The man looked up from warming himself by the fire. 'Why are you doing this, sir?'

'Because I can,' answered Sir William, and moved towards the door. 'No one will die from the potato blight on my land.'

Outside, John asked him 'How many more are you going to look after, sir? All your cottages and sheds are nearly full.'

'When all the sheds are full I'll start to bring them into the house.' They walked to the kitchen door of the main house where Maud was busy helping their cook prepare huge pots of stew. 'That apron suits you, Maud,' laughed Sir William. Maud smiled, adding more meat.

'Oh, by the way, the locals think you've lost your mind.'

'I have, Maud, and it's such a wonderful feeling that I intend to lose it again tomorrow, and the day after, and the day after that, till this the potato blight is over. No one will die on my land.'

'That's all very good, William, but we will soon run out of food at this rate, and then we'll all be headed for the grave.'

'We are going in that direction every day, Maud.

'Yes, but dear, we are the only landlords in Ireland who are helping the poor, and we are close to ruin ourselves!' Maud said, feeling exhausted. Sir William didn't reply, but studied his wife carefully. 'I must say that I underestimated how good you would be in the kitchen, dear.'

'I didn't know there was so much suffering,' Maud said, sadly.

Just then, John appeared. 'Sir, the locals are very thankful that you've opened up your property for those in need,' he said. 'Word has spread as far as Londonderry, and a wealthy stranger sent word this morning that he wants to donate as much food as you need to feed the forty-five families that you have taken in.'

Sir William turned, and John could see that his eyes were red. 'I was sent here to look after the Crown's interests and what can be more important to the Crown than its people. We are all the same. We are born the same way and we die the same way. It makes no difference.' He paused. 'John, I never told you something. My grandfather came from Ireland.'

John looked surprised at what he had just heard. 'Now I understand, sir,' he answered, looking fondly at his master.

Chapter 15

Thomas had sent word for the lord to join them on a return trip to the valley. He wanted to show him the new map and suggest a new development. Lord Shrewsbury's coached arrived at the cottage just as Thomas and Richard were finishing their breakfast cup of tea.

'Great day for a trip up the valley, gentlemen,' the lord shouted from the carriage window as Thomas and Richard grabbed their equipment.

'It's always a fine day in this job, sir,' replied Thomas, stepping up into the coach. 'We have one of the best jobs in the land, sir. Every day we get to see parts of the country that most people don't even know exists.'

'True Thomas, and I hear that you meet very interesting people too.' He gave a hearty laugh, Thomas looked at him sideways, and smiled. He was now seated opposite the lord but still felt uneasy. Then Richard joined them.

'I think I might approve, Thomas,' said the lord, bending forward in his seat to look Thomas in the eye. 'However, I need to talk to you and find out more about your past and, so long as things progress slowly and in the right way, I might just give my approval.' Thomas was flabbergasted! He could hardly speak. How much had his daughter told him, he wondered.

'Have you got the new map with you, Richard?' asked the lord, changing the subject.

'Yes, sir,' stuttered Richard. and began to unfold it.

When they arrived at the scenic spot Thomas took a few deep breaths. 'I've got a suggestion, sir, that you may or may not like,' he said, pointing at the far end of the valley. 'I've looked very closely at the whole geological setting here, sir. and it came to my attention that someone has asked to build a generating weir at the rivers exit down there.'

He paused, unsure of the next suggestion. 'I was wondering how you might feel if you were to suggest to the authorities that, instead of a small generating weir, you build a huge damn and flood the entire valley. There would only be one family to rehouse, and the scenery wouldn't change that much. The dam would generate enough electricity for perhaps even four counties and would earn the estate enough revenue to avoid selling any more land for business or housing. If it were built correctly, it could also become a public water supply to the whole county.'

There was a long silence, and Thomas couldn't tell by the lords face if was pleased or not. He stood and looked down the valley for about five minutes before he turned to Thomas and replied. 'What a clever idea, Thomas! Jolly good thinking there, lad. Do you think it would really work? The cost would be enormous to the government, and they might wish to proceed with their original plan instead.'

'We've studied the end of the valley. sir, and it narrows naturally, which means the dam wouldn't have to be long; just deep. I believe our calculations are right, and the benefits far outweigh the cost.' He turned and shook Thomas by the hand and then gave Richard a pat on his back.

'Gentlemen, what a clever idea!' He turned back to look down the valley. 'I can see the sun setting over the new lake, and it could be even more beautiful than it is now.'

The journey back seemed longer to Thomas as his emotions were in turmoil. He stare silently out the window for most of the journey to the cottage. 'Tonight you dine with me, gentlemen. Seven thirty sharp.' The lord announced loudly, as they left the carriage.

There were just the four of them for dinner at the main house. Christina tried to be very calm but her eyes were shining with happiness. The lord was in usual jovial form and made fun of Thomas's reaction to him finding out about Christina, and Richard was enjoying the slight awkwardness in the room, frequently kicking Thomas under the table. Christina was impatient to talk with Thomas alone.

They were about to start their desert when Edward marched in. He took one look at the four of them dining together, and scowled. 'Another meal which excluded me, I see.' He left, slamming the door loudly.

'My apologies for my son, gentlemen,' said Lord Shrewsbury, as he poured Thomas more wine. 'He has never got over the death of his mother, and blames me for everything. Sad, as he was once a very happy young man.'

Christina looked embarrassed, and said softly, 'We all miss my mother, but we don't behave like that.' The lord changed the subject and returned to his usual jovial self.

'How much more do you have to do, Thomas?'

'We're actually getting on a lot faster than my boss anticipated, sir, and I would expect we should have the project complete in ten months instead of twelve. However, I'm not sure what problems may be in store for us in mapping the west side.'

'Take your time, gentlemen. I would rather have the map one hundred per cent accurate than done in a rush, and I cannot wait to show the local engineers your plans for the dam.'

The rest of the evening was taken up with small chat until, out of the blue, the lord said, 'Richard, come with me till I give you a tour of the house. I'm sure Christina and Thomas need some time to discuss things.' There was an awkward silence. Nevertheless, Richard followed the lord out the door.

Christina went straight over to Thomas and sat down on his knee. 'My father really likes you,' she said, looking very happy.

'I just can't believe how fast this is all going, Christina,' Thomas said, looking into her deep blue eyes. 'It all seems like a dream. Maybe I'll wake back in Ireland just in time to cut the turf.'

'What's 'turf'?' she laughed.

'Turf is what we burn on our fires in Ireland instead of wood and coal. Here you call it 'peat.'

'I would like to go there some day, Thomas.'

'It's a sad place right now, Christina. A lot of people are dying because the potato crop has failed - but maybe someday.'

She kissed him passionately, with hardly time to take a breath. Thomas couldn't resist and, at first, made no effort to control her. Then he sat up suddenly. 'Hold on Christina. Imagine what would happen if your father came back in.'

She seemed agitated. 'It will take them hours to go around the house,' she said, 'but if you don't want me, then that's all right.'

'I do want you, Christina, more than anything else in the world, but let's keep this for a longer time together.'

'What do you mean by that, Thomas?' she asked sharply.

'I just thought that, maybe, if your father agreed, we could get married.' Christina threw her arms tightly around his neck.

'Yes! yes! I'll marry you.' Just then, the lord and Richard came in. They sat down opposite them. 'Thomas has something to ask you, father.' Christina announced, nervously. Thomas felt as if he was in front of a firing squad with minutes to live. Christina put her arm through his and squeezed it.

'I ... was wondering, Lord Shrewsbury, if it would be possible to ...' He glanced helplessly towards Christina. 'I would like to marry Christina, sir,' he finally blurted out. There was silence for a long time before Lord Shrewsbury turned to Christina and Richard.

'Leave us please for a minute. I need to talk to Thomas alone.' Christina looked annoyed, but grabbed Richard's arm and led him out of the room. 'Tell me about your life, Thomas, and why should I allow you to marry the most precious possession I have in this life?'

'I don't believe I am worthy of your daughter, sir,' began Thomas, walking over to the fireplace. 'I don't deserve any of this, and I feel like if I go to sleep tonight that tomorrow I'll wake up back in my land as a poor farm worker.' Lord Shrewsbury handed Thomas a glass of brandy and stood beside him.

Over the next half hour, Thomas related his story. When he finished, there was a long silence. Then Lord Shrewsbury spoke.

'Why do you want to marry my daughter, Thomas?'

'I've never felt this way before, my lord, and I fell in love with Christina when I first saw her in the woods. I've since learned that she is a wonderful woman with a deep sense of what is right in life. It's as if some outside power has brought us together.'

'If you had known her mother, son, you would understand why she's so easy to love. Christina is all I have left in this life, Thomas. Will you promise me you'll love her and keep her safe?' Thomas sat down beside Lord Shrewsbury, and now had tears in his eyes. 'Sir, I'll look after her and love her till the day I die.'

'Well, that wasn't too hard was it, lad?' The lord jumped out of the seat and shook Thomas by the hand. 'I see no reason why my beautiful daughter should not marry someone who she is obviously in love with; a clever young man who, I believe, will look after her till the day she dies.'

'Christina!' he called, knowing she was waiting outside the door.'

As Christina came into the room, her father smiled, 'Well. Say hello to your future husband, my darling.' Christina ran to her father and hugged him. 'Oh, Daddy, Thank you! Thank you! Today you have given me all that I've ever dreamed of.'

Richard sat staring as if he was watching a play at a theatre. Trying to compose himself, he stood up and said quietly, 'It's getting late, Thomas. Maybe we should let Christina talk to her father now.' Lord Shrewsbury showed them to the door. 'I'll see you tomorrow, gentlemen. God speed.'

Thomas and Richard walked back to the cottage in silence until they reached the door. Then Richard turned to Thomas and said sadly. 'From this moment, everything changes.'

Thomas looked at him in the eye for a few seconds and then said kindly, 'everything will change, Richard, but you, my friend, will be part of it.'

Chapter 16

The next day Thomas and Richard set off in a cart, rather than a carriage, as they planned to go down a track in the woods that led to some rough ground. They had gone about a mile when they heard several shots nearby. Thomas stopped the pony and turned to Richard.

'Did you hear that?'

'Yes. I noticed Edward and Malcolm earlier walking into the woods with rifles. They're probably out shooting birds.'

'Strange place for shooting birds, Richard,' remarked Thomas, but thought nothing more of it. As they turned a corner in the woods they came to a clearing where Thomas had reckoned they would need to use as a way point for measuring the next piece of land. He dropped down from the cart as Richard reached into the back to get their equipment. Suddenly there was another loud shot and Thomas felt a searing pain in his chest. He collapsed onto the ground. Richard looked in the direction the shot came from and saw two men running away.

'Thomas!' Richard screamed, as he bent down. 'Thomas!' He lay lifeless, and blood was pouring from a wound in his chest. 'Please no! Thomas don't go! Don't go!' He pulled his head up. He was limp and silent.

'No! No! Thomas please! Stay with me!'

Richard knew he was a long way from help, so he lifted Thomas and put him in the back of the cart. He jumped up onto the front seat and started the pony back down the track as fast as it could go. The tears were streaming down his face and he whipped the pony to make it go faster.

At the end of the track he turned left and soon found the drive to the house. As he reached the front door he screamed for help at the top of his voice, at the same time ringing the front door bell. Soon the butler opened the door and Richard told him what happened. A few minutes the later Lord Shrewsbury appeared and took control of the situation. They lifted Thomas out of the cart and carried him into the house.

"Fetch the doctor! Quickly now!' shouted Lord Shrewsbury to one of his staff. 'Bring him back here. Hurry!' He got Thomas into one of the many spare rooms and tried to stop the flow of blood that was already soaking the bed. 'How did this happen?' The lord asked Richard as he stroked Thomas's head.

'Two men came out of the trees down near the lake and shot him, sir.'

'What two men Richard? Did you see them?' Richard looked down, reluctant to answer.

'Which two men, Richard?' The lord now shouted angrily.

'I think one of them may have been your son, sir' he replied very reluctantly. The lord looked at Richard and knew he was telling the truth, but didn't want to believe it.

The doctor arrived an hour later and started working with Thomas while putting everyone else out of the room. Lord Shrewsbury took Richard down to the study where he poured them both a very large glass of whiskey. At that moment, Christina burst into the room.

'Where's Thomas? Where is he?'

'He's been shot, my darling, and the doctor is with him now'

'Shot! Where? Was it an accident? Who did this?' she screamed. Where is he now?

'You can't go to him, Christina. The doctor is trying to save his life.

'What happened to him? I need to see him!'

'Two men in the woods shot him' he stated nervously. The lord motioned to him behind Christina's back not to say any more. He didn't want him to disclose the identity of the assailant.

'Why?' she cried 'Why on earth would anyone want to shoot Thomas?'

They all waited impatiently for half an hour before the doctor emerged from the bedroom.

'I'm afraid the wound which Thomas sustained is very serious,' he said quietly, putting his bag down on the table. 'The bullet entered his shoulder, but part of it just missed his heart. I've stopped the external bleeding, but I've no idea if there is still some internal bleeding. He has gained consciousness, but is in a lot of pain. I've packed the wound in hope there will be no infection, but the next twenty-four hours will be critical. He must have complete rest, and his dressings must be changed twice a day. I shall return shortly. We shall do what we can to save him.'

With that he picked up his bag and left the room. There was silence, until Christina began crying loudly. 'It's so unfair. I have only just found my beloved and someone has now taken him away from me!'

'He hasn't gone yet, my love. He's a strong man. He will pull through.' Lord Shrewsbury said gently.

Richard was about to leave the room when the lord told him that he was to stay in the house tonight for his own safety in case the two men would come looking for him. Christina tried to find out from Richard who the men were, but he gave nothing away. He went outside and brought the cart around to the back of the house.

As he walked back to the front door, a police carriage pulled up and several officers got out and went into the house. He decided that it was best to wait outside, but one of the butlers called him inside. The police officers were talking to the lord in the drawing room when he entered.

'This is Richard, officer. He was with Thomas when he was attacked,' said Lord Shrewsbury, as Richard entered the room. 'Tell the police men what happened Richard.' Richard went over his story very carefully as the police asked him the same questions several times until they were sure that he had identified the right men.

'Thank you, Richard,' said the lord, as he opened the door for Richard to leave.' If you go into the kitchen downstairs cook will get you a sandwich to keep you going till dinner time.'

'No thank you. I won't eat until I know that he's out of danger.'

The next morning, the doctor came back and went straight upstairs to Thomas. When he entered the room, he was surprised to see him sitting up talking to Christina.

'I said he was to have no visitors,' said the doctor gruffly.

'I'm not a visitor, doctor,' replied Christina, smiling 'I am his fiancé!' The doctor didn't reply, but began examining Thomas.

'Wait outside please, miss,' he said, as he began to examine the wound. 'You're a very lucky man. The bullet went so close to your heart that you were a hair's breadth off breathing your last.'

'It's hard to kill an Irishman, doctor,' Thomas joked.

'You'll live young man, but you're going to have trouble using your left arm. The muscles in your shoulder have been torn by the bullet, and it'll take a long time, if ever, for them to recover. I may presume that because you are sitting up and colour has returned to your face that the internal bleeding, if there was any, has now stopped. You must rest, as the wound close to your heart must heal. If not, you could collapse and die very quickly. Do you understand?'

'Yes doctor,' replied Thomas, smiling, but closing his eyes. 'I'll rest now.'

The doctor came down the stairs as Christina and her father came out of the drawing room.

'I think he'll live,' he said, in a very matter of fact tone. 'He needs rest - alone.', he said, looking at Christina. 'It'll be weeks before he'll be able to work again, sir, but he should make a full recovery.'

The doctor headed for the door just as the doorbell rang. The lord didn't wait for the butler, but opened the door himself to show the doctor out. Two police officers were standing outside, and Lord Shrewsbury brought them in to the hallway. 'We have arrested the two men, my lord,' the policeman started. 'They're in custody and have confessed to the crime.'

Lord Shrewsbury was about to ask them to talk quietly so that Christina wouldn't hear, but it was too late. She was standing right behind him.

'Who are the two men?' she demanded.

'Edward Shrewsbury, your brother, and his friend miss,' he replied quietly.

Christina turned to her father, asking accusingly, 'You already knew this?'

'I did, sweetheart, but I didn't want to tell you yet.'

She slumped down into a nearby chair. 'My brother tried to kill the man I am hoping to marry! She sobbed. 'Why? How could he do such a thing?' she cried. Lord Shrewsbury took her into the lounge and made his apologies to the policemen. Richard appeared from upstairs and talked briefly to the policemen,

'What will happen to the men? he asked quietly.

'Edward will be tried for attempted murder and his friend, as an accomplice. They might both hang or, if not, they'll be locked away for life.'

'Does Lord Shrewsbury know that, sir?'

'Yes, he does. He's the one who gave us the tip-off as to where we might find them.' Richard walked away wondering how he had got himself involved in such a complicated life.

Lord Shrewsbury knocked on Thomas's bedroom before entering. Thomas was sitting up looking out the window. 'I'm most dreadfully sorry, Thomas." The lord began, as he took a seat beside the bed. He looked down at the floor, and it was the first time Thomas had seen him genuinely sad. ' I cannot believe that my son would do such a thing; and that to my future son-in-law, as well!' Thomas remained quiet as he knew the lord's heart was breaking.

'I didn't see who shot me, sir.'

'Richard saw them, Thomas, and the two have confessed. I've no doubt that Edward will be found guilty. He will most likely hang. I love my son, even though he stopped loving me a long time ago. Edward believed that Christina would inherit the entire estate, you know. That has all changed now. Tomorrow I will change my will to leave my estate to Christina. I never thought life could change so quickly, but with one foolish act of greed it has changed forever.'

'I don't deserve your kindness, my lord, and I think that when I can walk again I should leave and return to Southampton. I've caused all this sadness for your family,' Thomas choked.

'No, my son. You have caused nothing but happiness to my daughter for the first time since losing her mother. Please, you must stay and look after her.' Thomas's mind was racing. He turned back to the window.

'My daughter loves you, Thomas, but I need to know for certain, do really love her?'

The question troubled Thomas. He frowned and thought for a few seconds. 'I love Christina more than anyone else in the world, but I fear I've brought unhappiness to your family and maybe it is better that we part, and I return home now, sir.'

The lord looked at him then said quietly, 'Thomas, you are the only man that I would want for my daughter and so I would ask you to consider your position carefully as you recover. Good day, Thomas.' Thomas was alone again, and his mind was racing so fast he thought his brain was going explode. Everything had now changed.

Chapter 17

Christina and her father were finishing their breakfast when the door opened and Thomas walked in. 'What are you doing Thomas?' exclaimed Christina, jumping up. 'You shouldn't be up!'

'I couldn't stay one more day in bed. I need to get out into the air. Besides, it's a wound to my shoulder, and that doesn't stop me walking.' laughed Thomas.

'Yes, but the doctor said you were to rest for a few weeks, Thomas, not six days,' replied Lord Shrewsbury.

'I feel fine thank you, sir. A bit on the sore side, but fit and healthy otherwise.'

He sat down and picked up a piece of Christina's toast, pouring some tea.

'You look better, my love,' said Christina, moving up to him. 'I thought I had lost you.'

'I thought that for a few minutes myself'.

'The ordnance survey company management were asking about you and wished you a speedy recovery and, in the meantime, they have sent another man to help Richard,' said the lord, rising from the table. 'They're amazed at the progress you have made,'

'Richard is very good at his job, my lord. I hope they don't think that I've managed this all on my own.'

'That's very modest of you, Thomas. I'll talk with you later.'

'What a mess I've caused, Christina.' Thomas said, with true sadness in his eyes, as hugged her.

'No Thomas, please don't think like that, my love. Father told me what he has already discussed the estate with you. It means that if we get married then you too will inherit the estate. We can have a wonderful future together – and our children.'

'I know Christina, that's what bothers me.' He paused and took her hands. 'I don't deserve you, or this. It isn't mine, and I feel like I'm stealing it from your brother.'

'Who tried to kill you?' she interjected sharply.

'I know, I know. But maybe he didn't mean it. Maybe it was just intended to scare me away.'

'His friend confessed that he had been planning it for weeks and intended to get you out of the way.'

Thomas looked at her closely. 'I was taught all my life by my parents that revenge only makes you a prisoner, Christina, so I do not wish him to die for this.'

'He may not die, Thomas, but he'll have a very long time to think about what he has done to our family.'

Thomas stood up. 'Take me to the garden, please. I need some air.'

They walked over to the fountain where they had first kissed and sat in the same spot.

'Why would the most beautiful women in the world, who has everything, ever want to marry a poor Irish man who has nothing, Christina?' Thomas asked, as he stared at the flowing water.

Christina took his hand and clasped them in hers, looking fondly at him. 'I don't want anyone else in the world but you, Thomas, because all I see is kindness and love. I've never seen that in a man's eyes before. Other men have looked at me and I know their intentions are not honourable, while with you it is as if we were born to be together.'

'I just don't feel that I am worthy of you and this life Christina. Maybe I should go home.'

'Thomas, fate brought you here to me. There's no doubt about that. I needed a kind and understanding man who would look after me.' She stroked the hair out of his eyes. Thomas put his hand on her cheek. ' I am the most blessed man in the world because you have agreed to marry me', She hugged him tightly for a long time.

'I'll marry you Thomas - on one condition: We must be together for all eternity.'

'Sounds wonderful, my love.' With that, they kissed again.

Thomas spent the next two weeks taking long walks with Christina as he built up his strength again. Richard and the new man worked hard to finish the project around the dam. The government engineers were delighted with Lord Shrewsbury's idea of flooding the valley, and approached the central government departments for funding to start the project. Lord Shrewsbury decided not to have any more dinner parties for a while as he was both sad and happy and wanted to have time to adjust to losing a son to prison and a daughter to marriage.

He suggested that the wedding be held in August while the weather was still nice. Thomas and Christina decided that they would have a small wedding in the local church with just close friends and family. Thomas knew that his own family could never come, especially as things were so bad back home. He asked Richard to be his best man and Christina asked two close friends to be her bridesmaids.

Lord Shrewsbury and he had talked about what would happen after the marriage, and the lord had insisted that Thomas would train to run the estate. He would have to give in his notice to the ordnance survey company just before the wedding. He asked the lord if there would there be a position for Richard on the estate as he had proved to be a loyal friend and clever worker. He agreed, and offered him a job as the estate foreman. Richard was absolutely delighted with this new position, also with the fact that he could remain in the cottage in the country and be near Thomas. He would remain his closest friend.

Sir William and Maud were exhausted. They sat by the kitchen table staring at their empty plates and the dwindling fire. 'So that's it William,' sighed Maud. William looked up at his wife, who he was now so proud of, and wondered at how the last few months had changed her from an aristocratic bore into a kind and generous helpmate.

'That's it, Maud,' William replied wistfully. 'We've done our best.' He poured tea into his cup and looked at Maud's tired dirty face. 'Every shed on the land is now full. How many did you count altogether?'

'Forty-five families; about two hundred people, including the children,' replied Maud sadly. 'That's all.'

'It's two hundred people who would have died, Maud, and some day, when this the potato blight is past, they will remember your kindness.'

'They may be here for some time, William. We must raise more money to feed that many. Did you hear anything back from London?'

'Only that there's plenty of food in England for those who can pay for it. They don't seem to realise how bad things are here or, if they do, they don't want to know, and, what's worse is that crops of potatoes and grain are still being exported from Ireland to England.'

Maud got up from the table and came around and stroked William's head. 'You're a good man, Sir William Campbell. England doesn't deserve you. Maybe we should just stay here in Ireland.' William looked up with surprise and smiled.

'Maybe we should.'

The wedding of Thomas and Christina was held on the 20th August in a small local church with only one hundred guests. They had both agreed that a lavish wedding was not appropriate, considering the sad state of Thomas's home country, as well as the recent events which had taken place on the estate. It was a simple affair, but full of love and laughter, and though it was a small wedding, it certainly was not lacking in style. Lord Shrewsbury had made sure there was no expense spared for his only daughter's big day. He had the church decorated like a grand cathedral and musicians hired in from all over the country. It was still hot that year and the reception was held in the garden overlooking the lake.

Strangely, however, the last few nights before the wedding, Thomas' mind had drifted back to Donegal and he found himself thinking about Mary. He remembered her kiss, the day he promised to marry her and their happy times together. He had taken out the cross Mary had given him and gazed at it for a long time, sighing. But then she up and left for America! What could he do?

Where was the God she talked about, he wondered? Could he not have looked after them without her having to leave her home and family? It was different for him - being a man. Her God had abandoned Ireland, anyway, he thought, as he had tossed and turned many nights. Anyway, Mary was like a sister, not like Christina, whom he loved.

Richard questioned him many mornings over breakfast as to why he was getting up and pacing the house at night. He had grown more troubled as the day of the wedding got closer and, instead of looking forward to the big event, he would often ask Richard if he thought that he was doing the right thing. Richard, knowing that both their lives depended on the wedding, assured him that he was certainly doing the right thing and that pre-wedding jitters were quite normal.

So now he was married. The light was starting to fade as the couple drove off in the finest coach that Lord Shrewsbury kept for very special occasions. It would take them to the station where they would get the train to Scotland for their honeymoon. Lord Shrewsbury stood long after the guests broke up and stared after the carriage, knowing he was saying goodbye to his only daughter whom he loved so very much. Richard stood behind him.

'They make a fine couple, my lord,' Richard said quietly.

'They do, Richard, but that does not make the pain any less.' Richard turned and started to walk back to the house.

'Tomorrow Richard,' called the lord. 'Tomorrow we'll go and see how the dam is progressing.'

'Very good, my lord. I'll organise that for the morning then.' The lord turned, and Richard could see that he had tears in his eyes.

'Thank you, Richard. You're a good man'

Chapter 18

The next day was another warm day with blue skies and a sparkling sun. The valley looked even more beautiful than usual as Richard pulled the open trap over to a view point. He took a pipe out of his tweed jacket and relaxed, contemplating on how his life had changed. He had joined the ordnance survey company on an apprenticeship from school and he thought he would be there for life. Everything changed when this Irishman from Donegal was hired, and that without even an interview or a test.

Thomas had changed his way of looking at life and, for the first time in his career, he learned what it was to have fun while doing his job. He had never met anyone like Thomas before. He was exceptionally clever, yet easy going, even while engaged in important projects. He was always telling him that life was too short to be in such a hurry.

Thomas had told him how that, at eighteen, he had nearly drowned, and from that point his life had changed. He was a mystery to Richard and, even after these few years of friendship, he felt he still had not discovered everything about this man.

Richard was still relaxing when Lord Shrewsbury's coach arrived. 'What a splendid morning Richard,' he said, taking his coat off and placing it back on his seat. 'How are feeling today after yesterday's celebrations?'

'I'm well, my lord,' laughed Richard, climbing off his seat. 'I didn't have too much to drink as I knew I'd be up early today.' Lord Shrewsbury stood by the edge of the ridge overlooking the valley.

'I still find it hard to believe that one day there will be a huge lake here, Richard. Are you sure this can happen?'

'I hope so, my lord,' Richard replied, handing Lord Shrewsbury a pair of binoculars. 'Have a look through these, and it will save us having to walk a mile down to the dam.' Richard showed the lord how to look through this new device and focus on the huge concrete structure that was beginning to appear at the ends of the valley.

'I am told by the chief engineer that the dam wall may take over a year to construct and then maybe nearly two years for the river to fill the valley, depending on the amount of rainfall each winter.'

'Hmm', replied Lord Shrewsbury. 'I can now see why the government wanted the land. Richard this is much bigger than I ever imagined.' He turned to Richard and handed back the binoculars. 'I should have charged them double, lad,' He joked. Oh well. I shall get free electricity from them after all this.

Lord Shrewsbury turned to go back to his coach. 'I have to go to London later, Richard, and I shall be away for a few days. It will keep my mind off my daughter and all that's taken place, so I shall leave you in charge. Just make sure the house is one piece when I get back.'

'I shall do my best, sir' replied Richard closing the carriage door 'Have a good trip my lord and try not to worry about Christina. She has found a good man.'

'I know, Richard, but my family is getting smaller every month.' With that he told his driver to drive on, and the coach headed back up the narrow dirt track to the coach road at the top of the hill. Richard walked back to his trap and proceeded to check some maps.

Lord Shrewsbury's coach came to a junction after four miles, and the driver took a right turn, a short cut that would lead them to the main road to the station. He had asked him to drive faster to try and catch the early morning train to London. The track was rough, and the coach lurched from side to side as the driver tried to avoid deep holes and branches.

They came to an area where the track passed through half a mile of thick forest with a small lake on the left hand side. As the driver turned a corner he was forced to jerk to the right as a deer was standing in the middle of the track. In doing so, the carriage caught a large stone and suddenly overturned, throwing the driver down the bank into the lake. The horse bolted, but was still connected to the carriage, but after a few frantic pulls got free and ran down the track. The carriage rolled again, and this time followed the driver down the bank until it was lying upside down at the side of the lake. There was silence.

Richard decided that there was nothing he could do by the dam as all the survey work was complete and it was now up to the engineers to make sure Thomas's drawings were followed very accurately. He turned his trap and headed back to the house. When he came to the fork in the road he stopped. He was due to turn left, but for some reason he felt that he should take the longer route back by the village.

Richard drove the horse slowly as he knew this track was not well looked after and, after all, there was no hurry on this beautiful day. He came to the forest and stopped to load his pipe. Looking down to his left at the lake, he was horrified to see a coach lying upside down by the water. Jumping hurriedly off, he tied the horse to a branch of a tree running quickly down the slope.

Richard felt sick in his stomach when he realised that the coach was Lord Shrewsbury's and, looking to his right, he saw the driver lying face down in the water. He pulled him out by the back of his jacket, crying. 'Are you injured, sir?' Turning the driver's head around he realised he was dead. 'Dear God, no!' he moaned. 'Lord Shrewsbury, are you all right?'

Richard ran to the coach and tried to open the door, but it was jammed tight. The coach was half full of water. He kicked the glass window so he could see in, and saw Lord Shrewsbury lying slouched on the roof. 'Lord Shrewsbury! Hold on! I'll get you out!' he yelled, shaking from head to foot. He grabbed a broken branch and prised open the carriage door. Grabbing the lord by his shirt collar, he pulled him out of the coach. He held his head in his arms and patted his cheeks, tears cascading down his cheeks.

'Lord Shrewsbury! Wake up, sir! It's ok, now. I'm here.' Lord Shrewsbury opened his eyes slowly and looked at Richard.

'Richard, tell Christina I love her more than life.' He gasped. 'Tell her she ...' Now silence.

There was no response as Richard felt for a pulse. He now realised that he, too, was dead. He just sat cradling the lords head in his arms, sobbing. Ten minutes passed before Richard finally stopped crying and realised he had to go for help. He dragged both bodies away from the water and climbed slowly back up the hill to his horse.

Upon entering the village, he went straight to the police station to tell them what happened. The police officer was a kindly country man who could see that Richard was traumatised and, instead of taking him back to the scene of the accident, got another officer to escort him back to the estate. Richard could hardly speak, and was totally overwhelmed as he considered the responsibility that would now be placed on his shoulders.

Upon recovering somewhat from his shock, he heard the policeman explain to the butler what had happened. They were also discussing how they were going to contact Thomas and Christina. 'No one knows where they're staying. They've gone to Scotland for their honeymoon, but could be anywhere,' said the butler. 'Thomas mentioned to me before he got married that Christina always wanted to visit Edinburgh, but as to where in the city they might be, I have no idea.'

'I'm sure there are many hotels in Edinburgh, sir. It may be very hard to find them.' The officer said to Richard.

'There may not be many hotels in Edinburgh, officer, that would be up to Christina's standard, so I would suggest that you start with the grandest and work down.' Richard said before adding. 'I need to go and find them and tell them what has happened. I honestly don't know how they'll cope with this latest news!'

'Sir, I would suggest that you leave that to the police You've been left in charge of Lord Shrewsbury's estate and we will need you to be here,' the butler said, sternly. Richard said nothing and left the room.

Thomas and Christina had just finished a late breakfast on their second day of their honeymoon and were standing on their balcony looking over Edinburgh city. 'What shall we do today, my wonderful wife,' asked Thomas, putting his arm around Christina's shoulders, 'unless you just want to go back to bed?'

Christina smiled back at him, and in a seductive voice replied, 'and what would be the matter if I stayed in bed all day with my husband?'

'Nothing at all, my love,' Thomas said laughing, 'but I thought you wanted to see the city.'

'The city can wait,' she replied, dragging him back into the room.

Christina began unbuttoning Thomas' shirt when there was a knock at the bedroom door.

'We didn't ask for room service,' she said, slightly annoyed, as Thomas went to the door.

Two policemen were standing there.

'Sorry to bother you, sir,' said the older policeman. 'Would you be Thomas and Lady Christina Shrewsbury, newly married daughter and son in law of Lord Shrewsbury?'

'Yes.' answered Thomas, alarmed. 'Is something wrong?'

'May we come in please, sir? We have some bad news for you, I'm afraid.' Thomas moved to the side and let the officers into the room.

'What's wrong, Thomas?' asked Christina, quickly pulling her shoes back on.

'Can you sit down please, ma'am,' asked the policeman quietly. Both Thomas and Christina sat on the bottom of the bed and held hands, bracing themselves for what was to follow.

'I'm afraid I've got some very bad news for you,' he said, solemnly, removing his hat. He pulled a chair over to the bed and sat down facing the couple. 'Christina, your father has been involved in a very bad accident with his carriage.'

'Oh no!' cried Christina. 'Is he injured?'

'I regret to inform you, ma'am, your father didn't make it. He passed away today.'

'No!' cried Christina leaping from the bed. 'What do you mean? He can't be dead! You've made a mistake!' Christina screamed.

Thomas jumped up and held her tightly as she tried to run out the door. 'How did this happen, officer?' asked Thomas, trying to hold Christina.

'We aren't sure yet' replied the younger officer, but it looks like the driver may have been going too fast at a bad corner and the carriage overturned and went down into a lake.'

'Please let me go, Thomas!' screamed Christina 'I've got to go to my father! He's not dead! He can't be!' Thomas hugged her more tightly as she tried to run out the door.

'Sir, the police sergeant said quietly to Thomas, 'We were told to escort you both to the train station.'

'Thank you, officer. Please give us a few minutes and we will be with you,' Thomas replied, unsteadily. The two policemen squeezed past the couple and left them in the room together. Thomas took Christina in his arms and lifted her onto the bed. 'My love, we must pack quickly and get ready to go. We need to catch the next train home, Christina.'

Christina lay on the bed, face down, sobbing like a child. 'Why, Thomas? Why my dear, sweet father? It can't be Thomas! I'm certain they've made some horrible mistake.' Thomas grabbed the two suitcases and started packing their clothes.

It was a long train journey from Edinburgh to Southampton, and Christina just stared out the window, crying unconsolably. Thomas wondered what lay ahead for them. He thought about the implications of Christina now becoming Lady Christina; inheriting the entire estate - that he would now have to run on his own! Strangely, his mind suddenly drifted to thoughts of sitting by Kinnego Bay in Donegal with Mary - when life was so simple. It seemed like a whole different world that now seemed so far, far away - and gone forever.

Chapter 19

Richard was busy organising the return of the two bodies. He felt totally out of his depth dealing with police and he felt that the staff of the house were well aware of the fact that he had no real authority there. He hadn't slept all night and skipped breakfast.

The butler came and asked him questions that he was unable to answer, when the doorbell rang. The same police officer who had talked to him the day before was standing on the doorstep.

'We have found Lady Shrewsbury and Thomas,' he started 'in the most expensive hotel in Edinburgh, as you suggested. They're presently on the train here and should arrive at ten thirty tonight. Maybe you could arrange for one of your carriages to collect them.'

'Yes certainly,' Richard replied, without hiding his relief. 'Thank you, officer. You did well to find them.'

'We have also examined the coach and it seems that the left wheel came off after hitting a large stone in the road. It may, or may not, have been speed related, it's hard to tell. Either way, with the driver now deceased, we may never know the full facts.'

'Thank you, officer. I'll pass all this to Thomas tonight.'

The carriage was waiting for Thomas and Christina at the station, and Richard stood on the platform as the steam train pulled in. The driver helped the couple with their cases, as Richard hugged them both. 'I'm so sorry Christina,' said Richard gently. Christina just held his arm and said nothing while Thomas walked beside him carrying one of the small cases.

Eventually, Thomas spoke. 'How could this have happened, Richard? His coach was the safest in the land.' He asked quietly.

Richard recounted what happened, adding, 'There was nothing I could do.'

'Good man Richard, I'm sure you did your best.' He turned away from Christina and spoke softly 'She's devastated. We need to get her home quickly.'

They reached the carriage and climbed in, while the driver put the luggage in the boot.

'You found Daddy, Richard,' Christina asked softly. 'Was he still alive?'

'For a few seconds only, my lady. The last thing he said was, "Tell Christina I love her".'

Christina now cried uncontrollably, while Thomas held her tightly.

There were a lot of people at the house when the carriage arrived, as word had spread fast. Many of Lord Shrewsbury's close friends and a few distant relatives turned up to find out what had happened. Lord Shrewsbury's brother, Henry, was in the lounge when Thomas and Christina came in. Christina ran to the arms of her uncle, while Thomas spoke to a police sergeant who was just leaving.

'Thank you so much for your help, sergeant. Your men did a splendid job of locating us in Scotland. Thankfully I had given Richard some idea of where we were going. Christina wanted no one to know.'

'It would appear, Thomas, that this has been a tragic accident, and at this stage we are not pursuing the events any further. I believe the undertaker will be bringing the remains home tomorrow, and if there is anything else we can do to help please let me know.' The sergeant shook his hand and left.

Thomas turned to Richard 'Well, my friend, what are we going to do now?'

'We?' enquired Richard in a quiet voice. 'You are now lord of the estate - and I am going to bed.'

'You are my number one man, Richard, I'm going to need you more than ever now.'

'Well, I think working for the ordnance survey company was a lot safer and simpler.'

'Go on to bed sleep, then, and dream of measuring poles, and when you wake up tomorrow morning be thankful that your life with me is never boring.' Thomas patted him on the shoulder as he turned and walked out the door. Thomas sighed. 'Life in Donegal was so much simpler than this' he muttered to himself before Uncle Henry came over and shook his hand.

The next few days was a mixture of business and sadness as preparations got under way for what was expected to be a very large funeral. Thomas was amazed at the type of people who came to the house, which included senior members of the government. They were very surprised to find a young Irishman in charge of the house.

The funeral was held at the cathedral in Exeter as there was no church big enough anywhere near the estate, and Thomas felt very out of place with so many English dignitaries in attendance. He did his best to comfort Christina, but to no avail. She was inconsolable. What worried him the most was the fact that she would hardly speak to anyone and didn't want anyone fussing over her. Nothing would ever be the same again.

Sir William opened the front door of the house just as a grand carriage pulled into the front driveway. He knew it was his good friend from Londonderry, who was a wealthy business owner.

'Good to see you George' he said, shaking the man's hand as he stepped out of the carriage. 'What brings you to these poor parts of the country?'

'Hardly poor, William, in these fine grounds,' laughed George.

'The surroundings disguise the reality very well. George.' Sir William mumbled. 'Anyway, to what do I owe this unexpected visit?'

'I've heard about the wonderful work that you and your good wife are doing, William, and, despite what you think, I've been touched in a heart that you might not think I even possessed.

'On the contrary, my friend. I have always known you to be generous with your employees, George, by building them houses and all that.'

'Look,' answered George, impatiently. 'I want to help you in the work that you are doing.'

William stood silently wondering what was coming next. 'I own six cottages five miles up the road in the Culmore area. They are presently vacant. I want you to have them, old boy, to accommodate some of your guests.'

William was shocked, and was about to say something, when George continued. 'What's more, I wish to donate money to your feeding programme. I brought a cheque with me.'

George reached into his coat pocket and produced the cheque. 'Spend it as you will, William. However, I have one request. Please do not tell anyone the source of this donation.'

'Two hundred pounds!' exclaimed William, looking at the cheque in amazement. 'That's a huge sum of money George.' George was already climbing back into his carriage and waved back at William.

'God bless your work William,' he shouted, as he closed the door.

Sir William walked quickly back into the house calling out to Maud. She appeared from the kitchen, covered in flour from baking. 'Look what George Kincaid has given me!' said William, waving the cheque at Maud. 'Two hundred pounds towards feeding the poor!' Maud was speechless, and was about to cry, when William continued, 'Not only that, but he has given us six cottages near Culmore so we can house the rest of our people.'

'There's hope for these folks yet, William. I thought we were going to run out of food this week.' said Maud quietly. 'God bless him.'

'I am going to go back to Mrs. Sweeney, Maud, to see how they're faring. I know they have their own house and land, but I sensed they were struggling when I saw them last. I have a grand house for them now if they'll only accept it this time.'

Sir William and John approached Rose Doherty's cottage, slowly dismounting at the end of their lane. The house looked well cared for and there seemed to be plenty of vegetables growing in the field beside the house. Martha came out of a new shed at the right side of the house with a goose and some chickens following her. She stopped and stared at the two men as they approached.

'Is your mother in, young lady' asked Sir William kindly, noticing the girl's strange behaviour. Martha just stared at them and said nothing. Rose suddenly appeared at the door. 'Take the chickens around the back please, Martha' she said, walking up to the two men.

'What can I do for you gentlemen' she asked politely.

'Are you Mrs. Sweeney, ma'am?'

'No sir. I'm Rose Doherty. Bridget Sweeney, who lives with me, is out the back digging up some carrots.'

'I'm Sir William Campbell from over the hill ma'am. I would be very obliged if I may have a quick word with Mrs. Sweeney.'

Rose turned and walked towards the left end of the cottage. 'Bridget!' she called 'You have visitors.'

Almost immediately, Bridget appeared with a bundle of carrots in her arms. She recognised Sir William right away. 'What do you want?' she asked, tersely walking up to the men.

'I know you've no reason to trust or like me Mrs. Sweeney for the terrible thing that I did to you some years ago, but I would like to make amends, if you will allow me to apologise.' Bridget was silent, as she could feel Rose listening just behind her. Rose had taught her that to forgive was a better way than revenge, and that not to forgive was to keep one in a prison for life.

'I've asked you before, but I would like to offer you and your family a new house for the one I took from you.'

'That's a very generous offer, Sir William, but I've made my home with Mrs. Doherty and Martha, and we are fortunate to have some land and animals to keep us. We have both lost husbands, and now our son and daughter, so it would seem that God has brought us together to look after one another.'

'I know about your husbands and your son, madam' Sir William said, with compassion in his voice. 'A most shocking and sad event, but I didn't know about your daughter.'

'Yes. Rose's daughter left on a ship for America and we haven't heard from her since. We have no idea if she's even still alive.'

'When did she leave, and from where did she travel?' asked Sir William concerned.

'Two years ago - from Londonderry.'

'Two years without a word?' Sir William asked in surprise. Sir

William looked at John and then turned back to Bridget. 'What is your daughter's name, Mrs. Doherty.'

'Mary' replied Rose, sadly.'

'I shall see what I can find out for you and, in the meantime, if either of you need any help, please call at my house.' Bridget and Rose watched them turn and walk back to their horses and ride off.

'That was the best way to deal with them,' started Rose. 'I'm proud of you for not taking his head off.'

'The thought had passed me by for a second, Rose, but I knew you were listening. Besides, your God was watching,' she smiled.

'He's your God too, Bridget, and you are as loved as I am.'

Sir William and John entered the grounds of the estate. William had not talked all the way home, but now he turned to John. 'Tomorrow John you must go into Londonderry and check the passenger lists for a Mary Doherty who may have gone to New York on one of McCorkell's ships.'

'I will, sir. It does seem strange that they haven't heard from her.'

'Yes, strange indeed John, but it is now my mission to find her.'

They dismounted at the front door, and John took the horses to the stables at the back of the house. Maud was waiting for him in the lounge. 'Well, my good man, how did that go' she asked tentatively.

'They seem content and well cared for in their own cottage, Maud,' William replied, taking his big coat off and throwing on the chair. 'I'll leave them to it, I think, till they come looking for help. Their daughter, Mary. went to America two years ago and they have not heard from her since, though. I'm going to try and find her for them.'

'Two years, William!' Maud replied in astonishment. 'Good luck with that, dear. She could be anywhere – dead or alive.'

Sir William rang the servants' bell and asked the maid for a cup of tea. 'I wonder how long we'll be able to afford out own staff, Maud, let alone feed all these families,' he said, sadly.

'I heard from your friend, Wallace, today,' Maud announced, sitting down on the soft sofa, 'that the government might be going to ease up on collection of our back taxes, as they know many landlords will lose their estate if they pursue these insane policies.'

'Wallace would know, Maud. He has friends in high places but, honestly, I can't see them changing their policies in a hurry.'

John came looking for Sir William in the garden when he couldn't find him in the house, but he was nowhere to be found. He decided to check the stables. Sir William was kneeling in one of the pens stroking the head of the old horse his farm hand had bought at the auction.

'What's wrong, sir?'

'The old thing is dying, John. Sadly, his time is at an end.

'He must be a fair age, John, and has done a lot of work in his life.'

Just then the horse moved his head to look at William for a few seconds, and collapsed, taking its last breath.

'I since found out, sir, that the horse belonged to Mrs. Sweeney, who lost her house. Her son, Thomas, brought it to the auctions where the farm hand paid more than the going rate.' John bowed his head 'He thought it might help them, so he gave them three pounds instead of two.'

Sir William stood up and looked at John in the eye. 'It would appear John that there are some decent people in the world, after all. That's what I would have done, too. Now let's see about moving him.'

'Oh, by the way, Sir William,' said John, moving out of the stables. 'I made enquiries at the harbour in Londonderry.' He paused 'I actually found a man who remembers Mary boarding the ship two years ago. He remembered because he said he had never seen a more naturally beautiful girl in all his life.'

'Good work John, and what else?'

'He said that she bought her ticket on her own and was waiting to board the ship when a man joined her. It seemed like he was escorting her up the gangway.'

Sir William looked very alarmed 'That does not sound good, John. Did the man know who this gentleman was?'

'No sir, but what concerned him was that he had seen this man take the ship on several occasions, which meant he had travelled back to Ireland a few times.'

'Right John. You've done well. Well, it's time I called in a few favours. I don't like the sound of this at all,' he said, shaking his head as he went inside.

Chapter 20

Thomas and Richard met for breakfast in the dining room. Christina was still in bed. 'How is she, Thomas?' asked Richard as he finished his eggs.

'Still not good, Richard. She's still extremely traumatised and dreadfully low. I'm beginning to wonder if she'll ever get over it.' They were interrupted as Henry entered.

'Good morning, gentlemen. Please don't get up.' He walked over to the far end of the table.

'Thomas, I've asked your chauffeur to take me to the train, if that is all right with you. I've got to return to Bristol, as I have a lot of work to do.' Henry continued, as he poured himself a cup of tea and sat down opposite him. 'Thomas, I need to make a few things clear to you about the estate, and there is no easy way to do that, so let me put it bluntly.' He paused and smiled politely at Richard.

'As you both seem to be involved in the estate, I suggest that you stay and listen too, Richard.' Richard stopped eating and put his knife and fork down, while looking apprehensively at Henry.

'When Christina married you, Thomas, my brother informed me that he had changed his will so that the estate would be left to her, and then, obviously, to whom she would marry. He cut Edward out of will entirely as he's likely to spend the rest of his life in prison – that is, if they don't hang him. However, there's a clause that states that if Christina becomes mentally incapacitated in any way during her first year of marriage, then the estate will be left to me. Legally, it's quite clear that Christina may only inherit the estate and title if she is of sound mind and in good health.'

Henry walked over to the table and put his cup down. 'I'm very concerned about the mental state of my niece and I don't believe she's in any condition to make rational decisions about anything, let alone about his estate that has been in our family for four hundred years. I've decided to give her a few months to recover and, if she isn't better during that time, I shall have no other option but to claim the estate as mine. I will then decide what to do with it. If she recovers well before that time, then the estate will be legally Christina's - but only after I am convinced that all is in order.'

Thomas stood up and faced Henry. 'She will recover, my lord. She's very upset now, but she will recover.'

'I hope so, Thomas' Henry said, making for the door. 'Believe me, I have no wish to take on this huge estate with all its financial burdens. Well, I'll be off now. Good day to you both.' Henry closed the door behind him and Thomas and Richard looked at each other, shocked. There was silence. The butler came in and asked if they needed more tea, but Thomas dismissed him with a wave of his hand.

'I wonder if I could get my old job back with the ordnance survey company,' Richard said, with a worried tone in his voice.

'Don't even think like that,' replied Thomas tersely. 'A few minutes ago, you were telling me that Christina would be all right, and now you're planning your retreat!'

'I'll go and see him off.' said Richard heading for the door.

Thomas opened Christina's bedroom door quietly and sat down on the edge of the bed. She was lying on her right side staring out the window. Thomas stroked her hair gently. 'How are you today, my sweetheart?' he started nervously. 'I miss you, downstairs.' There was no reply.

'It's been two weeks now since the accident. It isn't good for you to stay up here.' Thomas paused and stroked her bare arm gently. 'Your daddy wouldn't have wanted you be like this.' There was still no reply, so Thomas sighed and stood up again. 'If there is anything you need Christina, just call me.'

Richard was busy loading equipment onto the trap at the front door when Thomas came out.

'Any sign of her coming round Thomas?' he asked, as he closed the door on the trap.'

'I'm now sick with worry about her, Richard. This isn't normal, and if she does not recover, she could lose everything.'

'We need to keep working then, Thomas, because if her uncle is serious, then it would be better for us if we had this project completed at least.'

'I'll come with you Richard. I've got to get my mind off her for a while,' Thomas said, as he climbed up onto the front seat of the trap beside Richard. They set off towards the dam.

Sir William was chatting to a couple of local people who he had re-housed in one of the stables when he saw John passing through the stable yard. 'John' he called after him 'I was looking for you.'

'Yes, sir, I was checking on the horses.'

'Excuse me folks,' Sir William said, turning away from his guests. 'I've got a very important job for you, John.' He put his arm around John's shoulder. 'I've contacted an old friend in New York and he's going to help you find Mary Doherty.'

'How can he help me, sir?' replied John with curiosity. 'He's in America, and I'm here.'

'Precisely John, and that is why I would like you to go to America to assist him. If you find Mary, you must bring her home.'

'America, sir?' queried John, in surprise. 'How on earth would I get there?'

'The same way everyone else in Ireland is getting there, John - by ship. I have already booked your ticket on the ship leaving Londonderry next week, and my friend Alfred will meet you in New York.' John tried to speak but was so shocked he couldn't get the words out. 'I shall give you two months, John, and if you haven't found any trace of her, then you must return home.'

They walked towards the back door of the house and Sir William gave John another pat on the back. 'There's no other person I would trust with this task, John, and I believe you'll find her.'

'May I ask you why, sir?' asked John, as William approached the doorway.

He turned and looked long at John. 'I don't sleep well at night thinking about how I was responsible for putting Mrs. Sweeney and her son out of their house two weeks after losing their loved one. I owe it to their friends who they live with to find their girl.' With that he closed the door. John walked off shaking his head in disbelief.

Thomas and Richard sat drinking wine in the evening sunshine overlooking Christina's favourite garden. The noise of the water from the fountains seemed louder this evening as everything was so quiet. Thomas looked at Richard, who was filling his pipe, and was sorry that he had got his friend into his crazy life.

Suddenly they heard a noise behind them and they both turned to find Christina standing behind them! They both stood up, and Richard could see both shock and relief in Thomas's face. 'I suppose dinner's over,' said Christina, as she walked up to Thomas and gave him a hug.

'It is, my love, but for you I'll order anything from the kitchen.' He glanced down. 'You've got so thin Christina. We must get you food quickly.'

'Let's sit for a while, gentlemen, while I take in what I've missed.' She sat down beside them and breathed the evening air into her lungs. 'I am so sorry for the way I behaved. The shock of losing my daddy nearly killed me.'

'It was an enormous tragedy, my love,' replied Thomas, with tears in his eyes. No one can blame you for being so upset.'

'How long have I been in my room?'

'Six weeks Christina.'

She just stared at the water and cried gently. 'It's time to live again, Thomas. Then she laughed. "And by the look of you two, it's time for a stiff drink and a jolly good meal.'

Thomas rang a bell on the table and the butler appeared. He ordered drinks and food for Christina. Richard walked down the steps to let them have some time alone.

'I thought I'd lost you, my love,' he said, with a broken voice. 'I thought that someday we would walk into your room and you would be gone.'

'I've never been so low before, Thomas. I was very frightened.' She sat down on his knee. 'It was the shock of suddenly losing my daddy - and so soon after such a happy day with him, and all. He was so proud of us.'

'Your father was the kindest man I've ever met, Christina, and now you must live life as he would want you to. You need to continue to spread kindness and laughter to others, just as he did.'

'I could never do that Thomas. He was one of a kind.'

'I know, my love, but that is what he would want you to do.' They kissed for the first time since their honeymoon, and suddenly life seemed to return to them both once again. Thomas stood up and poured two glasses of wine, handing one to Christina. He clinked his glass against hers and said, 'Let us start again then, my love.'

'Yes, Thomas. We will find our way again.'

Chapter 21

June 1846

John stood on the starboard side of the ship as it moved slowly into New York harbour. The crew was busy folding all the sails while it made its way by steam for the last part of the journey. The sea crossing from Ireland had been long and traumatic, as many sick people had died. As the ship pulled into the harbour, John breathed a sigh of relief that he had survived the gruelling journey.

He stared at the high buildings that seemed to reach to the sky behind the port sheds, and already he could sense the excitement of everyone around him who came for a new life. The crowds soon gathered on the quay to watch the Irish ship come in. The passengers were now all lining the decks eager to see a place that looked like heaven on earth in comparison to the misery from which they had just escaped.

John went below to fetch his case from his cabin, while everyone rushed past him carrying their entire life in sacks and tattered suitcases. By the time he got on deck, most of the passengers had already disembarked, and John looked for the man who was to meet him. As he stepped off the gangway, a man in a customs uniform stepped in front of him.

'Name?' he asked, abruptly.

'John Montgomery,' replied John. 'House manager to Sir William Campbell of Donegal.'

The customs man looked down at his ledger and nodded. 'Yes, I see, sir. What is your destination and what is the purpose of your visit?'

'I don't know my destination, officer, as I'm being met here by a police officer called Lieutenant O'Hare who is to help me find a person of interest to his lordship.'

'Over there,' motioned the customs man as he pointed to a door in one of the offices. He stepped aside, and John pushed ahead through the crowds.

As he reached the door of one of the offices he felt an arm grab him from behind. 'I presume you are John Montgomery from Ireland.' the man shouted above the din of the hustling crowd of passengers. 'I'm Lieutenant O'Hare from the New York Police Department.'

'I'm very glad to meet you, Lieutenant. I was beginning to worry about getting out of here.' John shouted back.

'Ok. Let's get you out of this place,' replied the lieutenant, pushing his way through the throngs of people. They reached the side of the huge shed and there was a police carriage waiting for them. As they pulled out of the harbour area, John could at last relax. Lieutenant O'Hare enquired politely about his trip.

The carriage had been travelling for about twenty minutes, and John was completely overwhelmed with the wealth he could see all around him. Street after street of fine buildings and grand shops, with occasional parks where people were relaxing in the autumn sun with their children. 'This girl, Mary, from Donegal, John. Tell me about her. She must be highly important for a British peer to send you all the way here to find her. What's her story?' asked the Lieutenant.

'It's a bit embarrassing for him, sir, but basically he feels he owes it to the friends she lived with after he evicted them from their cottage - by mistake.'

'Sounds a bit strange, John, but then most of the English do,' he laughed. 'Still, I owe him a favour. Did you know that I worked for him twenty years ago?'

'Really? He never told me about the connection' John said, surprised.

'It's a long story, but I was working for him in England and he helped me get a job with the police here. He supplied me with an excellent reference.' John went quiet as he knew very little about Sir William's life before he came to Ireland.

'I've checked The Custom's list of immigrants, and your Mary arrived here on the 19th of September 1843, on the ship 'Erin' from Londonderry.' He paused and looked at John closely. 'After that,' he said slowly, 'she completely disappeared.'

'Oh, that is strange, sir,' replied John. 'She isn't the type of girl to run off and not write to her mother at home.'

'Are you aware of what's happening to the Irish here right now, John?'

'No, sir, I'm not,' replied John, sounding concerned.

'You may just call me "Alfred", he said, smiling.

'In a few minutes we'll be passing a place called Five Points. It's called that because five roads meet at one junction. It is the poorest area of New York, and it is also where all the Irish live. The prosperous people of America have forgotten their Irish roots and there seems to be no compassion here to help new immigrants, including those who have landed from Ireland. They're treated the same as native Africans and live in dire conditions. Many of my colleagues try to help them, but many of them eventually just drift hopelessly into a life of crime and debauchery.' John looked shocked. He looked around and could now see the area that Alfred was talking about.

'If Mary came over here on a ship on her own and disappeared then it's quite likely she has been kidnapped and used by men. There are men who travel back and forth on that ship and look out for girls who are travelling on their own, or even with a family. The men appear to be very friendly, promising to help the girls find work when they get here, but they end up in brothels. Many of them only last a year before they die from disease, in childbirth or through malnutrition. Most are never heard of again.'

'I can't believe Mary would be that foolish, Alfred. She's a very strong girl - and moral. I doubt very much that she would fall for that type of persuasion.'

'It isn't persuasion, John, it's kidnapping, and the people behind it are very clever. They give the girls new names and documents and threaten them not to tell anyone or they'll be killed. We've found many bodies of young women who have obviously been discarded by the men who used them and left to try and survive on the streets or of those who tried to escape.'

John shook his head and dropped his eyes to the carriage floor. Alfred could see that he had seen enough, and ordered the driver to change route. 'I thought everyone was rushing over here to America to find a new life and prosperity,' John said sadly.

'Those folks who land here with a bit of money and contacts seem to do well enough, John, and many travel further west.' Alfred pointed towards the harbour. 'But sadly, those who come with nothing and have no friends end up in Five Points and may take a long time, if ever, to leave it. Americans here don't want any immigrants, but especially Irish, as they have caused a lot of trouble in the past. As I said, they seem to have conveniently forgotten that they're all immigrants.' Alfred saw how shocked John was and decided he had seen enough.

'I'll drop you off at your hotel, John, but take my advice. Don't enter this area on your own, or you might never be seen again. We don't go in there unless we have a squad of men with us.'

'Where should I start, sir?' asked John, very perplexed.

'It could be a very long process, but you never know what you might find. I would start with every hospital within the city and ask to see the admission records. If they become difficult, show them this card. I would also try every hotel, guest house and pub as she may have got a job - if she escaped. It's unlikely that she would be employed by a shop, as they don't employ immigrants. Finally, and as a very last step, check the cemeteries,' he said darkly. 'She may have already left us.'

The police coach stopped outside a small hotel on a side street, and Alfred opened the carriage door for John.

'Thank you, Lieutenant. You've been very helpful.' They shook hands as John turned towards the hotel door.

'Take care, John, and good luck with your search. If you start with the supposition that she is already dead, then you may get some good news if she's still alive. Any problems contact me at my station.'

The hotel was dreary, and the paintwork was brown and dark red. An elderly man smoking a cigar behind the reception desk handed the room keys to John without saying a word, even when John said a polite, 'thank you'. He was glad to get to his room, even though it was only lit by one small oil lamp. He pondered all the things that the policeman had told him, and was almost ready to give up before he even started.

The next day John walked out the door of the hotel into the summer heat. He had never been in such heat before, and felt suffocated in his heavy tweed coat. There was a younger man on the reception who, at least, acknowledged him and gave him directions to some of the closest hospitals. He felt a huge weight on his shoulders with the almost impossible task of looking for one Irish girl among so many people.

John noticed the city had a strange smell to it - and so much noise! No matter what street he turned onto there were carriages, carts and people, all rushing somewhere. He noticed that there was a municipal cart with men cleaning the streets of horse manure, and was surprised at how clean the footpaths were kept. He stopped to look in the windows of some of the shops. The array of goods on sale left him in awe and he compared these to the tiny shop windows back home in Ireland.

Twice he nearly got run over by carriages as he tried to cross busy road junctions, and so, by the end of the day, he was exhausted and deflated. He stopped at a diner near the hotel to have a meal. It was nearly closing time, so he had just time to eat his meal quickly at a table by the window on his own. A man at another table kept staring at him, and as he was about to pay his bill came up and sat opposite him.

'My name's Matt' he said in an American drawl, holding out his hand. 'You look a bit lost.'

'No, I'm not lost. Just a bit amazed at your busy city,' replied John warily. The man was wearing a sports jacket with a strange American hat. He looked tough.

'You're not from here, are you?'

'No, I'm from Ireland. I've come to look for someone,'

'Well you've come to right place as there are probably more Irish here than in Ireland, but who are you looking for?'

'A young girl in her twenties called Mary who came here two years ago.'

The man laughed 'Well you may as well go home, my friend, as there are thousands of 'Marys' here from Ireland, but tell me, why the interest in this one?'

John didn't reply, and he decided it was time to pay the bill and leave.

'We don't like people snooping about looking for 'Marys' here,' the man said, threateningly. 'Take my advice and go home.'

'I will.' John said, now annoyed. 'I'll go home when I find her. Good day to you, sir.'

'Be very careful,' he said as he walked to the door. 'This is a dangerous place for people like you.'

John went to the counter to pay his bill, where the waiter had been watching this exchange. 'Better not to annoy that man, you should know. He runs the gangs here and is a dangerous man to cross.' John thanked the waiter and left.

Chapter 22

Thomas met Richard at the far end of the estate, an area that had been neglected by Lord Shrewsbury. It looked beautiful in the autumn sunshine with rows of fruit trees and small fields with stone walls that led up and down the small hills and valleys. The only sound was the sheep bleating as they grazed in the meadows and the background noise of the small river lapping over the worn stones.

'Well Thomas this is it.' said Richard, as he wrote down some measurements in his surveyor's book.

'It is, Richard, and most of the work has been done by you my dear friend.'

'No. I owe you this wonderful life, and, believe me, I shall never forget it. Had you not taken me with you on this project, I would still be working for the ordnance survey company in Southampton, making maps all over England. Instead, I am now estate manager of six thousand acres and have a life that many a man would dream of.'

'It's strange how life turns out,' Thomas responded. 'Anyhow, let's get going. We need to get this final measurement done so we can be home for lunch. I'll post our last survey to Southampton tomorrow. They can count themselves lucky that we agreed to finish a project that we are no longer employed on.'

'Christina seems to be keeping better now, Thomas. I hope it lasts.'

'I think it will Richard,' Thomas replied, as he put the measuring poles into the back of their trap. 'It was a big shock for a young girl, and now to find herself Lady Christina with such responsibility cannot be easy.'

'Have you heard from her uncle Henry' Richard asked.

'Yes, he has signed off on the estate after Christina went to see him and now everything is hers,' Thomas replied, getting up into the trap.

'Not just Christina's, Thomas,' Richard smiled. 'You are now a very wealthy man.'

'I have no time for wealth, Richard - especially when I'm having to pay you vast sums of it,' Thomas teased.

As they pulled up by the front door a police carriage was already parked in the driveway and a policeman was standing talking to Christina. She called Thomas over to join her. 'This officer has just informed me that Edward's trial was concluded yesterday. He was found guilty of attempted murder.' Thomas just stared back without saying anything. 'The judge has sentenced him to life imprisonment.' Thomas remained silent. 'I believe, sir, that if you were to contact the judge and make an appeal, the sentence could be changed to hanging - if that is what you wish,' the policeman said to Thomas.

'I don't wish him harm at all, officer,' replied Thomas, moving to put his arm around Christina. 'We have had enough death for one year, and I hope he'll be released before too long.'

'That's very generous of you, sir, considering how he did try to kill you.'

'He was afraid he would lose everything - which now he has - and I think that's enough punishment for any man. Besides all that, he was influenced by the recent sad events which took place.'

'I'll leave that to you, sir. I'm only informing you of the final judgment, and I hope now you both will be very happy here.'

'Thank you, officer,' said Christina, 'There's no doubt we will.' The policeman got back into his carriage and drove away.

'Who's for a big lunch, gentlemen?' enquired Christina, more cheerily, as Richard joined them.

'A pint of your famous country ale wouldn't go amiss, Lady Christina,' smiled Richard, as they moved towards the front door.

'How's my daddy's estate, Thomas?' Lady Christina asked, as they walked into the dining room. 'It's looking good, Christina, and it is now your estate,' Thomas smiled.

'Our estate, Thomas. Daddy made sure of that.'

'I feel like I have no right to be here, my love,' Thomas sighed, as he sat down for lunch. 'I am a poor boy from Donegal who just happened to fall in love with the most beautiful woman in the world, and I feel like I've stolen you away from your own people.'

Christina sat opposite him, rebuking him. 'Thomas, I never want to hear you speak like that again! My father thought you were one of the cleverest young men he had ever met and knew you would be a kind husband to me. If he had had any doubts, he wouldn't have left the estate to us, so whether you feel worthy or not, the estate is ours and will be passed on to your son or daughter.'

The butler brought lunch and the conversation turned to lighter things.

John went to the front desk at the police station and asked for Lieutenant O'Hare. He shivered in the cold, even though it was a warm day. The place looked dirty and run down, and all the paintwork was different shades of green. He could see officers working in back office, and they all seemed very engrossed in their work. To his left he could see a prisoner being escorted down a long drab corridor and then pushed into a cell with a loud clang of the closing door. He was glad to be going home, even though his mission to find Mary had failed.

'My Irish friend,' said Lieutenant O'Hare, as he came to the desk. 'What can I do for you today?'

'Good day, Alfred. I just called in to thank you and to say goodbye,' said John, sadly.

'No luck in finding your girl then?' Alfred replied, with genuine concern.

'No. I don't believe it will ever be possible to find her now. I tried all the places you suggested and even more, but sadly Mary was nowhere to be found. We can only pray that she has found somewhere safe to work and that she'll go home one day. Life here is so completely different from life in Donegal. I'm surprised that anyone coming here could survive.'

'We're not all bad. my friend,' replied the lieutenant, laughing. 'Many a Donegal man has done well here'

'I'm sure that's right, sir, but perhaps not so many Donegal girls,' The lieutenant escorted John to the door and shook his hand.

'Sorry you had a wasted two months, sir, but I hope you have a safe journey home.'

John stepped out into the August heat and dust of the busy street. He walked the half mile back to his hotel as he wanted to experience the bustle of New York one last time before he would get his coach to the harbour. He turned right at the next junction into the quieter street, upon which his small hotel stood. The street still had a lot of people, all in a hurry to get somewhere. He passed a café with tables set out on the walkway where people were drinking coffee - something he had never tasted.

Just passed the café was a small guesthouse on the other side of the street. It was very well kept, and was unusual in that it was painted in bright pink and red. He wished now that he had stayed there instead of the drab hotel, where he had slept so badly for the last two months. As he looked in the open front door a maid appeared with a brush and started sweeping the doorway. John was dumbstruck! It couldn't be! He quickly crossed the street between the passing carriages and as he came to the front of the house he called to the maid, 'Mary!' The girl looked up in shock but said nothing.

'Mary Doherty,' called John, again.

The girl looked scared and turned to go back in, shouting behind her, 'I don't do that anymore'. She ran quickly into the house, closing the door firmly behind her.

John walked nervously up to the door. He was now sure that the girl was the Mary he had met with Sir William one day while on the horse. He pulled a bell cord and heard the bell ring deep inside the house. A few minutes later the door was opened by an elderly lady dressed in a uniform.

'I am sorry to bother you, ma'am,' started John, 'but I was sure that a maid working for you is the girl I've been looking for.'

'She doesn't do that line of work anymore, and you should be ashamed of yourself calling here for her. Good day, sir.' The lady went to close the door, but John put his foot in it.

'I have no idea what you are talking about, ma'am. My name is John Montgomery and I've come all the way from Ireland to look for a Mary Doherty.' The women eased the door open again and stared at John for a few seconds.

'How do I know you are not one of her clients who she so luckily escaped from? How do I know you're not here to try to drag her back to that despicable life?'

John reached into his pocket and produced his boat ticket and card from Lieutenant O'Hare.

'This is my boat ticket home to Donegal tonight, and this is the policeman who has been helping try and find Mary.'

'Oh. You'd better come in then, sir,' the lady said, as she closed the door behind him. 'I'll go and talk to her and see if she wants to meet you.' She turned to face John and spoke sternly to him. 'Do you even have you any idea what this girl has been through?'

'No' replied John. 'I've seen enough in two months, but I'm sure it has been worse than I could even imagine.' The lady looked at him, and walked down the corridor. A few minutes later she returned.

'I'm sorry, sir, but Mary doesn't want to meet with you, and I am not going to force her. Good day to you, sir.' She showed John to the door. Mary was listening by the kitchen door, her heart pounding.

'I was sent by Sir William on behalf of her family who have been worried sick about her for the last two years. They are also now finding it very difficult to run their farm without her. They will want to know why she isn't coming home and if she is being kept against her will.' John turned to look down the corridor and thought he could see the kitchen door slightly open. 'My ship sails on the high tide tonight and this will be her last chance to come home.'

'I'll pass that message to her, sir, but she has made up her mind to stay and work here of her own free will.' John looked at the woman and then turned and walked down the steps to the street.

He had walked about a hundred metres down the street when he heard a girl's voice calling him. 'Sir, wait!' John turned, and Mary came running up to him. She was crying.

'Please tell me! How is my ma, sir? How is Martha?'

'They're managing, Mary, but miss you terribly,' he said, with deep compassion, 'but they have been so distressed at not hearing from you. They even thought that you were dead.'

'I am too ashamed to go home, sir, after the life that I've lived, I couldn't bring myself to even think of my past till you came to the door. They wouldn't want to know me now.'

John took her hand that was covering her eyes and spoke gently to her. 'Mary, nothing that you've done will ever change the love of your family; in fact, to the contrary. If they knew what you've been through they would love you even more.'

Mary sank to her knees in the middle of the walkway, crying like a child. John knelt beside her and put his arm around her shoulders. 'I've got a ticket for you for the ship home, Mary, only you must come immediately.'

'I can't, I can't,' she sobbed.' John held her face gently and made her face him.

'This is your only hope to restore your life, Mary, and God has brought me here to bring you home.' He said firmly. She went quiet for a few minutes.

'You know, sometimes I felt that my God had left me, sir. I made a bad choice to come here and I thought He blamed me for my foolishness, but then again I know He rescued me from that horrible place.'

'I met Thomas as well.' John ventured, as they started to walk back to the house. Mary swung around at the mention of his name.

'Where?' she exclaimed.

'He came home from England to look for you, but you had already left for America'

'How was he, John?' she asked, as she started to dry her tears.

'He has done well in England, Mary, but he was very sad that you weren't at home, so he didn't stay long.'

They reached the door of the house, and John stopped, and grabbing her by the shoulders. 'Mary, please come home with me. If I go home without you, your family will be distraught. They're longing so much to see you again.' John pleaded, and then smiled, 'and Sir William will likely fire me for wasting his money.'

Mary stood, thinking hard. She was suddenly overwhelmed with thoughts of home and the happiness she had left behind. 'If I come, what will I tell my new family? They'll have no maid.'

Just then the door of the house opened, and the lady of the house stood and watched them briefly before walking towards them. 'Mary, it's time to go home,' she said softly.

Mary ran to her and gave her a hug. 'Oh, Ann. What am I to do?' She cried again. 'I can't leave you after all you've done for me!'

'You must, my child,' Ann replied, taking Mary's arms off her gently. 'We'll be sad, Mary, but we'll manage.'

John walked over to them both and said, 'Ma'am whatever you would pay Mary for six months I'll now pay you to release her so that you can find a new maid.'

'That will not be necessary mister. We don't need a new maid.'

Ann looked steadily into John's eyes. He moved uneasily, before saying, 'We'll have to go now if we are to make the boat to Ireland.'

'Go! Change quickly Mary,' Ann said, pushing her towards the door.

John and Mary got a taxi carriage that took them back to the hotel to collect John's bag before heading for the slow journey to New York harbour. They didn't speak the whole journey. Mary stared out the carriage window and John allowed her take in the sights of the city that had destroyed her life. Sadly, he watched her troubled face, thinking to himself, 'She will never forget'.

The taxi took them right up to the side of the ship, where they both collected their small bags before boarding. Mary was in a daze, and kept looking back over her shoulder as if expecting this experience to end suddenly. 'There are not many people going on the ship,' was all she said, as they climbed up the gangway.

'Not many people go this direction, Mary, as most people are leaving Ireland because of the potato blight. We will have most of the ship to ourselves.'

'The potato blight? What do you mean?'

'The whole potato crop of Ireland failed, Mary, and thousands and thousands of people have died already.' Mary was shocked and sat upright.

'How is that possible, John? Are my folks all right?'

'Yes, Mary. They're all right, but it's hard for everyone right now. You need to know that you're going home to a lot of sadness,' replied John, as they walked onto the ship.

Chapter 23

Thomas and Richard were discussing the new farming plans for the estate over breakfast when Christina came in and sat down opposite them. Picking up a letter, she asked cheerily, 'So what are my fine gentlemen doing today?'

Richard looked at Thomas, who smiled across the table. 'I thought,' announced Thomas, ' that since Richard has done such a splendid job of sorting out our tenants, we should all have a day off and go somewhere nice.'

'That's a lovely idea, Thomas,' Christina laughed. So where shall we go?'

'If we hurry we could maybe make a day trip to the sea and bring a picnic,'

Christina got up from the table and was about to go over to the window when she suddenly stopped. She groaned loudly, putting her hand on her stomach. 'I think I need to sit down,' she said, turning quite pale.

'What's the matter, darling?' Thomas asked anxiously.

'Never worry, dear. I'm fine. Just cramps from our large dinner last night, but perhaps a trip in the coach isn't a good idea today.' Thomas got her a glass of water from the table and crouched down in front of her.

'Should I call a doctor. my love?'

'No don't be silly Thomas I'll be fine.' Richard left the room and went out to the garden. 'I didn't want to tell you, Thomas, while Richard was present,' Christina said, smiling into Thomas's eyes, 'but I think I may be pregnant.'

Thomas suddenly leapt to his feet. 'Oh, my goodness, are you sure?'

'No, not certain, but fairly sure.'

'That's wonderful, darling! But why are you in pain? Do I need to call the doctor?'

'No, not yet. I'll wait another few days, but these cramps are very strange.' Thomas helped her from the chair and walked her towards the door.

'Let's get some autumn sunshine. It'll be good for you,' he said as they walked to the front door. Christina walked into the sunshine but just then, Thomas, having second thoughts, turned and went back into the hall. He called the butler over and gave the order to call their doctor.

John and Mary leaned over the port side of the ship as the deck hands loosened the ropes and cast off. A heavy cloud of black smoke billowed from the one funnel in the middle of the ship as the steam engines pulled the ship away from the berth. All of a sudden Mary panicked, looking frantically for a way to jump back on land. John grabbed her gently by the arm and tried to comfort her.

'I don't know what I am doing, John. I need to stay here!' Mary cried, with panic in her voice.

'No Mary,' replied John quietly. 'This was not the life for you. Your real life is waiting for you back home.'

'Is it, John? Is it? I don't know if I can face life back home after what I've done.' She started to cry. John hugged her. 'Believe me, Mary, it will be thousand times better than this.' They both turned to watch New York city begin to disappear as the ship left the bay. The men began to unfold the main sails that would help the ship cross the Atlantic.

'Perhaps we should go inside now, Mary. It's getting cold,' John said kindly. They went down a flight of steps and walked along a dimly lit corridor with flickering oil lamps. They came to a heavy door that led into a small canteen where a very large woman was dishing out the last of a pot of Irish stew. Mary sat down at an empty table, while John got two plates of stew and mugs of tea. They finished eating in silence. Mary was deep in thought and seemed nervous, but she seemed to relax slightly as they finished their tea.

'What ever happened, Mary? How did it all come to this?' John eventually ventured.

Mary stared at him for a long time then dropped her head, tears flowing once again. 'You must promise me, John, that you'll never tell my family what I'm about to tell you. I am only telling you because I believe you are a kind man who has taken the trouble to come and find me. Do you promise me, John, please?' she pleaded, with deep sadness in her eyes.

'I do, Mary, though I feel I must relate some of it, at least, to Sir William. You know, he has paid a very large sum of money to find you.'

Mary took a deep breath and began. 'When I boarded the ship in Londonderry two years ago, it was packed with all sorts of people leaving Ireland. I was on my own, and I looked for other girls my age, but most others were with family or their men folk. As I made my way onto the ship, a very nice man stopped me and asked after my health. I met him again the next day on deck and he asked me if I had contacts for work in New York. I said no. He then told me that his friends ran an organisation that found work for Irish immigrants. He seemed so kind that I agreed to come with him when we arrived in America.

When we arrived, and cleared customs, he introduced me to

another well-dressed man and they told me that if I went with him he would take me to a work centre where I could sign up for work and get accommodation. I had no one else to help me, and so I went with him.

The place he took me was a tall, rundown house with dozens of rooms on each floor. The man showed me into a dark room which had only one bed in it and a window covered over with a blanket. It was very cold, and when I asked him if there were any blankets he turned very nasty and said I wouldn't need many blankets with the type of work I was going to do. He had an evil smirk on his face when he said it. He left the room and locked the door on his way out. I began to realise that things were bad when I heard screams from a woman from next door.' She paused and began to cry again before attempting to continue.

'I was brought up as a Christian girl, John, and all my life I believed in God who loves and cares for us. My mother was a devoted believer, and so I had a sheltered life in Donegal. Do you know what I mean, John?' She held her head in her hands and could hardly continue.

'I fell asleep on the bed and didn't wake up till someone brought some bread and tea in the morning. I asked if I could get out, but the American woman didn't speak, and she just locked the door again when she left the food in. A few hours later the woman opened the door and showed a man into my room. The man forced me to undress and then forced me to do things with him. I tried to fight and force him off, but he hit me and forced me to do what he wanted. I screamed for help, but no one came. He left, and I thought I was going to die.

An hour later another man came in and did the same. By the end of the day, six men had been with me. I screamed and banged on the door till the woman came back and slapped me on the face and told me be quiet. She told me that this was my life now and that having intercourse with men meant I could have free room and food. I went to sleep crying that God would take my life or let me escape.' Mary looked up at John who now had tears coming down his cheeks.

'This went on for six months, John, until one day I got very sick and collapsed. They moved me to room with other sick and pregnant girls where we were left on our own to die, while new young girls were brought in to replace us. I became numb, John. I no longer felt any emotion. It was as if I had already died, but my body was still here on earth.'

'I cannot imagine what you went through, Mary, dear,' he said, wiping her tears. 'It sounds like hell on earth. So how did you finally escape.?'

'I had a fever for a long time and kept dreaming I was back in Donegal with my mum and my dear friend, Thomas. It may have been the fever, or it might have been real, but one night, Jesus appeared to me – perhaps it was a dream, or maybe it was real – but, anyway, he spoke softly to me and said, "Mary. I've heard your mother's prayers and I am going to set you free." When I woke up the next morning the fever had gone, and I felt a strange peace.

The horrible American woman came in with scraps of food for us and she began shouting obscenities at one of the other girls who was in the process of giving birth. Then she turned and ran out the room to get something, and she left the door open. I struggled to get to the door and found that the corridor was empty, so I ran for the stairs. There was no one on the stairs and I could see light at the bottom coming in from the front door. I ran down the stairs and out the door, expecting someone to grab me from behind, but they never did.

I soon found myself out on the street. I didn't know which way to run and I was so frightened! The street was crowded with intoxicated, rowdy men. I took a deep breath and ran as fast as I could. I fell many times and when some man smelling of liquor picked me up I slapped him hard on the face and ran even faster.

Eventually the street led to a cleaner area, with less people. I was hungry and thirsty, but I kept running - perhaps for a mile or two. I stopped at a water pump in the street, but the water tasted bad. As night came I really panicked. I passed the back of a hotel and went through the trash to see if there was any food. Can you imagine? I found half a loaf of bread in the bin and then curled up outside a door in a back street to eat it and tried to sleep.

The next morning, I woke up with the cold, and wondered how I could end my life. Just at that moment, a well-dressed man came out of the door behind me and saw me lying in his path. He bent down and spoke to me, but I could hardly hear what he said. He called for someone in his house and a lady came and helped lift me up. They took me into their nice house, brought me to a lovely room and put me to bed. I woke up in the evening with the lady bringing me a big dinner.

A little later the man came in and asked me my story, as he sat on the end of my bed. When I told him my story he had tears in in his eyes, and then I knew that he was a kind man. He told me that he and his wife owned the small hotel that I was in and that I could stay till I got better. His wife came in and said that they were Quakers and that they always liked to help people in need, as well as running the hotel. I didn't know what Quakers were, but was glad that they would help me. The women said that when I felt better that she might have a job for me if I wanted to stay.

Well, they kept their word, John, and they turned out to be the kindest human beings I have ever met. That's where I worked for a year and a half - until you came to the door.' Mary looked at John with very deep sadness in her eyes. 'You see John; I wanted to repay their kindness. That's why I didn't want to leave them.'

John was very quiet for some time before he cleared his throat, and asked, 'But why did you not write and tell your family that you were safe and well?'

'I am so ashamed, John, of what I did. I could never tell my ma, and I didn't ever feel that I was worthy to live in their house, or even set foot in Donegal again. I'll never be the same person again.'

John took Mary's hands and held them in his, as he looked her in the eye. 'Mary, none of this is your fault - none of it. You have nothing to be ashamed of. Those wicked men forced themselves upon you. You were not to blame for this! It was never your fault,' he repeated, gently.

'There were hundreds of men, John. I lost count. I am not a clean person any more. My soul has been taken from me,' she sobbed.

'No Mary. You are the same wonderful person you always were, and you can rebuild your life again'

'You're a very kind man, John. I wish I could believe you, but I can't.'

John stood up and helped her from the table 'Let me escort you to your cabin, you may feel differently when you see Ireland again.'

'Thank you, John, but I'll find my own way to my cabin. I'll see you in the morning - and thank you once again for coming for me.' She gave John the most grateful look he had ever seen in his life.

Christina was not very pleased when a carriage arrived at the front door with a doctor in it. 'Thomas' she said scolding 'I thought I told you not to call the doctor!'

'You did, darling, but I just want to be sure everything is all right.' They left the rose garden where they were enjoying the late afternoon sun and walked to the house.

'Wait out here,' Christina ordered Thomas, as she followed the doctor into the house. Thomas paced up and down outside the front of the house. Richard came around the corner and looked at Thomas.

'If you need to walk that much Thomas, why don't you walk to the lake?'

'Very funny, Richard. The doctor's in with Christina. She might be going to have a baby, or something.'

'Or something'? What do you mean 'something'? Great news, Thomas! You will be a father. I can hardly believe it!'

Thomas stopped and looked at Richard. 'Go and do something useful and give me some peace.'

Richard smiled at him 'Stop worrying, Thomas she'll be fine, but at your command I'll go and measure something - hopefully with liquid in it.'

Some time later the doctor stepped out the front door. 'Your wife needs to rest, sir - and rest properly,' the doctor said to Thomas as he opened the coach door. 'She has some early complications with her pregnancy, but she should be all right so long as she takes plenty of rest.'

'What sort of complications?' demanded Thomas, holding open the carriage door

'She will explain, sir' he replied as he closed the door.

Thomas rushed into the living room where Christiana was lying on the chaise lounge. She seemed upset. 'What's wrong, Christina?' he asked in a concerned voice.

'I'm going to have a baby, Thomas, that's what is wrong,' Christina answered.

'That's wonderful, my love! But the doctor said there was a problem. He didn't say any more. What can be wrong?' Thomas took her hands and looked into her eyes. 'What can I do Christina?'

'Stop worrying, my love. Everything will be fine.'

The next month seemed to pass very slowly for the three of them. Richard was so efficient that he managed to turn the estate around, and the revenue from its farms and new business interests began to increase. Thomas couldn't work, as he was preoccupied with Christina and her present condition. They both spent their days planning new gardens with waterfalls and long avenues of trees, and such like.

By mid October the evenings were getting shorter and the air much cooler. Thomas and Christina were walking back from the lake one evening as it was getting near dinner time when Christina stopped and turned Thomas towards her. 'Thomas.' she started gently. 'I want you to know that I've never been happier in all my life. I know that I've found the most kind and loving man in all the world. I want you to know that if anything was to ever happen to me, that both my daddy and I knew that you were brought here by someone up there.

I never told you how desperately unhappy and lonely I had been since my mother died, and even though Daddy was the best in the world, I knew I could never fit into the world into which I was born.' She paused and stroked his face. 'To have you in my life turned my night into day, my sadness into laughter and my loneliness into a beautiful companionship. You are the first person who really understands how I think.'

'Christina please don't talk like this. You're scaring me.'

'I just want you know this in case anything goes wrong with the birth of my child or I get sick.'

'That's wonderful, Christina, but you are going to be well and healthy. Soon we will have a family, and then you might not think me quite so wonderful. I'm a little scared about taking on the responsibility of fatherhood. I really want to be a good father.'

Christina kissed him hard on the lips, then laughed. 'You're right, Thomas. I shall be fine – and you will be the best father ever.'

Chapter 24

John found Mary standing on the starboard side of the ship as it entered Lough Foyle. The October morning air was chilly, but, despite the cold, she stood as if in a trance, staring pensively as the ship approached Greencastle, on towards Moville, and finally reaching Londonderry

'It will not be easy Mary' John said gently as he moved beside her. 'You're going to need a lot of courage.'

Mary didn't reply for some time. Finally, she turned to John and said, 'I've definitely decided that I won't tell anyone what happened to me, John, and I'm asking you again to promise me that you'll do the same.'

'I have to tell Sir William and his wife, Mary, or they may get rid of me for not telling them the truth but, apart from them, my lips are sealed.'

Mary went quiet and then turned and looked at John. 'They don't need to know everything, John, please.'

'It's cold this morning, Mary. Let's get our bags ready. The ship will be docking in an hour.' With that they moved to the stairs.

Impulsively, Mary turned to him and said gratefully, 'You are an angel in disguise to rescue me, John. I shall never forget you. Perhaps you were sent by God – I don't know - sometimes I wonder if I will ever again believe as I once did.'

The Derry port was very busy as the ship was tied up on the quay. Mary could see hundreds of people in a queue waiting for papers to board their ship. She wanted to run down and tell them what real life was like in America and warn any single girls about being kidnapped.

She knew that no one would believe her and would call her some names that she couldn't bear to hear right now, so she kept the pain in her heart.

There were cargo ships unloading grain and coal in a line all the way up the quay to the city centre and she suddenly felt a wave of release. She had made it home, and was now beginning to want to see everyone again. John helped her with her bag as they walked down the gangway. He showed the customs man their tickets and entry documents that Sir William had arranged for them, and soon they were climbing onto his carriage. The road home was taken in silence. Mary couldn't believe she was back in Ireland.

The carriage pulled into Sir William's estate. 'We have to change the horses, Mary, before I take you home,' John said, as he put his hat on. 'It won't take long.'

'I'll walk home, John. You have done more than enough for me, and I need time to think.' John could see the apprehension in Mary's face, and tried to reassure her, before he stepped out of the carriage at the front door.

Just then Sir William came out of the front door. 'John' he said, holding out his hand. 'I'm so glad you've made it back, my man. 'Very well done for finding this young girl!'

'Thank you, sir,' he answered with great pride. 'May I introduce Mary to you. She is one of the bravest girls I have ever met.' He opened the door so that Mary could climb out, but she stayed in the carriage. John motioned to Sir William that she was reluctant to get out, but she leaned forward as if she wanted to say something.

'I want to thank you so very much, sir, for sending John to America to rescue me. I cannot tell you my story, sir, as it's too painful for me, but John will tell you later. All I can say is that you've given me my life back. I shall be eternally grateful.'

Sir William smiled kindly at Mary and stepped back from the carriage. 'No, Mary. By helping you I hope that I have partly redeemed myself from any part I may have played in the eviction of your friends and neighbour. Now John will escort you home. I'm sure your family will get a shock - and a wonderful surprise!' Mary sat back as the stable man hitched on two fresh horses to the carriage.

The light was starting to fade as the carriage pulled up at the end of the lane leading to Mary's home. 'I don't know how to thank you, John, I'll never forget what you have done for me.'

John reached across and opened the door. 'I will never forget you either, Mary, as it isn't often one meets a woman of such strength and character. I pray that life back with your family will repay the immense sadness that you have been through, and that you know that not all men will behave like the ones you met in New York. I pray that one day you will find a good man who will always love you and protect you. It's best I go on now, Mary. God be with you.' Mary turned and kissed him on the cheek. John turned the coach as Mary walked slowly towards the lane.

Martha came out the door and spied Mary coming towards her. She stood in silence just staring at her sister whom she hadn't seen for nearly four years. Mary stopped and held out her arms. 'Hello, wee Martha! How are you, and how are the chickens?' Martha just turned and ran towards the house shouting, 'Ma! Ma! Mary's back!'

Just then her mother, Rose, appeared at the door. 'Mary!' She exclaimed loudly, wiping the flour off her apron. 'Mary, is that really you?' Rose ran to Mary and they both stood embracing each other;

tears running like rivers down both their faces. Bridget came from the back of the house and joined in the welcome. They all stood hugging and chattering furiously until Rose suggested that they go in for dinner and sit by the warm turf fire.

Chapter 25

Thomas and Richard examined a large map of the estate which they had received from the ordnance survey company, along with a letter congratulating them on such a detailed piece of work. 'They've done a great job, Richard,' said Thomas, patting him on the back 'but then they had the two best surveyors and map makers in the country.'

'Take care Thomas. Self praise is no praise,' he grinned.

'When the government pays the estate over the next few months there'll be enough money in the account to run this place for the next one hundred years,' Thomas said, and then sighed, 'It's so sad that Lord Shrewsbury didn't get to see it.'

'Yes, but just remember, Thomas, it isn't just Christina's, it's yours as well,' Richard said, folding up the maps.

'It may be, Richard, but I have no interest in it. If I were not married to Christina, then all I would be is a map maker. I feel like I've come over from Ireland and stolen something that doesn't really belong to me.'

'Don't let Christina hear you talk like that, Thomas. You would make her feel very insecure, especially as she is about to have your child,' Richard said, reproving him.

Thomas turned to Richard and spoke softly, but seriously. 'It's hard for you to understand, Richard, because you've never left England, but my heart still lies at home. One day I shall return and buy my mother a big house with hundreds of acres to try and compensate for what was taken from her.'

'Christina would never leave here, Thomas. This is her life,' Richard replied.

'Is it Richard? The reason she married me was to escape from this pretentious way of life and the people who flap around her. She might like Ireland - and so might you, my friend.'

'Funny you should mention home, Thomas. I've been thinking I might take a trip home to my folks now that the work's completed. There will be nothing here to do for a good few months.' Thomas was about to say something when the butler came rushing in the door.

'Begging you pardon, my lord, but you need to come now. Christina seems to be having difficulties.'

Thomas dashed to the door and ran up the main stairs in four strides before racing down the corridor to his bedroom. One of Christina's personal maids was at her bedside holding her hand.

'What's wrong?' Thomas enquired anxiously, sitting on the side of the bed. Christina opened her eyes and looked at Thomas. Her forehead was covered in sweat, and she was groaning with pain.

'Get the doctor!' Thomas shouted to the butler who had followed him upstairs.

'There's something badly wrong, my lord,' the maid said. 'Perhaps there's a problem with the baby. It could be coming too early.'

Christina screamed and tried to hold Thomas's hand. 'I'm with you, my love. Try and hold on now; the doctor will be here soon'

'Thomas, it's too late,' Christina cried, with a broken voice.

'What do you mean it's too late, Christina? Don't worry, darling. Everything will be fine.'

'No Thomas.' She grabbed his hand. 'Something is wrong.' she closed her eyes for a minute then screamed again. 'I feel so cold, Thomas.'

'What can we do?' Thomas yelled 'What can we do? Thomas grabbed a facecloth and started to gently rub Christina's face.

'Hold on, my sweet darling. The doctor will be here soon,' Thomas said with a cracked voice trying to conceal his fear.

'Thomas. I feel so cold. Please lie beside me, my darling,' Christina cried. Thomas lay down beside her with tears flowing down his cheeks. Christina opened her eyes again and pulled Thomas towards her. 'I love you, Thomas. You are everything to me,' she gasped, and then fell back on the pillow. Thomas grabbed her and tried to sit her up on the pillow, but she lay still.

'Christina, wake up!' shouted Thomas. 'The doctor is coming.'

There was no movement. The maid began to cry. 'I think she's gone, my lord,' she sobbed.

'Don't be silly. She has just fainted with the pain,' Thomas said with more confidence than he felt. 'Christina. I am still here, my love. Wake up now.' Christina had turned white with no movement in her body.

Thomas began to talk to her, as he had done many times, but there was no response. The nurse left the room to fetch Richard. When he rushed into the room he could see that Christina was deathly white, but Thomas was still talking to her. He went over and put his hand on his friend's shoulder and whispered, 'Thomas, I think she has gone, my friend.'

'No, no! She's just sleeping, Richard! She'll be awake for dinner soon.' Thomas cradled her in his arms and rocked back and forth, sobbing. The grim realisation of what had just happened was beginning to dawn upon him, but he wasn't prepared to face it. Not yet.

The doctor arrived an hour later in the estates coach and rushed up the stairs.

'I need everyone to leave the room please,' the doctor said firmly, 'including you, Thomas, please.' Thomas didn't argue. He was in deep shock, and Richard held his arm as they left the room.

The doctor emerged from the room a few minutes later with a grim look on his face. 'How long was Christina in pain before you called me?' he asked, Thomas.

'We don't know, doctor. It was her maid who found her in this distressed state and came to us right away.'

'I am afraid that she has passed away, sir, and' ... he hesitated, 'I regret to inform you - the baby also. However, without a post mortem I would say that the baby was already dead from some days ago.' Thomas sat on the top step of the stairs and stared out the long window.

The doctor then excused himself and suggested to Richard that he stay with Thomas.

'I shall make arrangements tomorrow to have Christina removed to the hospital for a post mortem', the doctor said from the bottom of the stairs. No one spoke. Richard sat beside Thomas with his arm around his best friend, both staring out the long window on the stairway.

Mary was stacking the turf in the shed at the side of the house before the December frosts came. Martha tried to help, but was making more work by stacking the turf the wrong way. Rose and Bridget watched her from the front door and spoke to each other softly.

'Whatever happened to my wee girl, Bridget?' Rose asked sadly. 'She won't talk about America at all, and it pains me to see her so changed.'

'Give her time Rose. She will some day, but you mustn't force her.'

'Why did Sir William spend so much money in bringing her home, Bridget? It seems very strange.'

'I would say that guilt may have played a big part in it, but I am not going to judge his kindness.'

'She won't stop working. It's as if she is battling something we can't see.'

'It's only two months since she came home. If she's still like this at Christmas, then you need to talk to her.' Rose was silent for a few minutes before speaking.

'I would like to travel to Sir William's house next week to thank him, Bridget.'

'Then I'll come too, Rose,' Bridget said, resolutely. They both went into the cottage to prepare dinner.

Sir William and Maud were having lunch in the dining room. Maud looked tired, as she had been working hard to help their new 'visitors'. The forty-five families housed in different parts of the estate had to be fed every day. Because of their own financial problems, they had cut the kitchen staff down to just one cook, so Maud had to help every day. William was proud of her, but concerned that she might lack the stamina to continue, at the age of sixty-five.

'One of the families came to me yesterday, Maud. They thanked us for our help but said that they wanted to return to their own home. It appears that the man was not reliant on potatoes alone and said it was time to get back on their feet,' William said as he finished his meal.

'I had heard that grain is getting into the county now, and seed potato, William, but I don't see how much of a difference that will make,' Maud replied, sighing.

'I read in the paper yesterday that over a half a million people have died already, but not from starvation. It appears when one is hungry the immune system is weakened and many people in the west have died from disease. It is truly shocking.'

'Why has the government been so slow to act, William? I hear there's no shortage of food in England,' Maud said angrily.

'Ireland has always been the poor relation in the Crown, Maud. It would have been better if it had been governed by its own people,' William sighed.

'Don't let any of our aristocratic friends here you talk like that, William. They would remove your title instantly!'

'They can keep it. What good has it done us except remove us from reality?' Just then the butler opened the door.

'Excuse me, my Sir. There are some visitors asking to see you at the front door.'

'Visitors?' enquired William.

'Just some people from over the hill, sir.'

'Right I'll come now.' Sir William stood up. 'We may have another family to replace those that are leaving already, Maud,' he said, as he went to the door. The butler opened the front door and two ladies were standing waiting.

'Good day ladies. How can I be of help to you?'

'You have already been of immense help to us, Sir William, and that is why we came - just to thank you,' Bridget said warmly. Sir William hesitated. Then he asked them to come into the hallway out of the rain.

'How have I helped you?'

'You sent one of your staff to find my daughter in America,' Rose said gratefully.

'Oh. You must be Mary's mother, then,' William said, embarrassed.

'Yes, I am, sir, and this is my friend Bridget, who now lives with me.'

'I am so sorry about your house, Mrs. Sweeney. I didn't authorise by bailiff to act like that. It was an outrageous act, and I must sincerely apologise and repeat my offer of finding you a new home, if you should want one.'

'There's no need to keep apologising, Sir William. It has turned out for the best, as my son, Thomas, went away to England and I would have been on my own, if it were not for Rose.' In spite of the awkwardness which he felt, William invited them into the drawing room. They declined politely and continued, 'We both just came to thank you for your kindness and to tell you that the whole community is talking about your relief work. They all hold you in high regard.' William didn't know what to say and just mumbled in reply.

'You are a good man, Sir William,' they continued, 'and we pray that God will bless you greatly for your kindness,' Rose said, shaking his hand. But now we must be home before it gets dark.'

'How did you both get here?' Sir William enquired.

'Just a wee walk over the hill, sir. We'll be home before dark.'

'Goodness, no!' exclaimed William. 'I mean ... no you can't walk that distance! I'll send for my coach'

'That won't be necessary, Sir William. We walked here, and we will walk home again,' Bridget said firmly.

'I'm sorry, but I cannot allow you to do that in this cold weather,' he said, going out the door. A few minutes later he returned, along with John.

'This is John, my estate manager, and he'll be delighted to drive you home, ladies.'

'We're so grateful to John for bringing Mary home,' Rose said kindly.

'That's all sorted then, ladies. Thank you for taking the time to come. May I wish you happier times in the future,' Sir William said, shaking their hands, 'and in future, should we meet, please call me William.'

John smiled as he escorted them to the coach, where a driver was waiting for them. He opened the door and helped Rose and Bridget into the coach and then, to their surprise, climbed in beside them.

It took nearly two hours for the horses to pull the coach over the mountain from Greencastle to Kinnego Bay. The first part of the journey was filled with small talk about the weather and the state of the country since the potato blight, and so on. However, just as the coach started down the far side of the mountain, John turned to Rose and asked quietly, 'And how is Mary, Mrs. Doherty?'

Rose looked at him for a few seconds before replying, 'She's alive John, thanks to you, but living is another matter.'

John was quiet for a while. Then he began to enquire further. 'I would say she is working very hard at everything. Would I be right?'

'How do you know that?' Bridget asked sharply.

'Because that's what she did in the hotel she worked at in America.'

'She always was a hard-working girl,' Rose said, defensively.

'But not that hard,' intervened Bridget.

'Has she told you what happened to her in New York?'

'No. She'll tell us nothing,' Rose said, sadly.

'I promised her that I would tell no one about anything if she came home with me, and that was the only way I got her to come.'

'The way she is now, John, it might have been better for her to stay in America.' John went very quiet and stared out the window. There was silence for five minutes, before he spoke again.

'Ladies, I feel it is my duty to tell you some things. I will tell you these only so that you can understand her better and try and help her; otherwise she might never recover.'

The women sat and stared at him as he related her story as best he could, sparing them the graphic details as much as possible. Both Rose and Bridget were in tears as the carriage was approaching their house. John finished by saying. 'You'll have to let her to tell you her story herself. If she's to recover, she'll have to realise that none of this was her fault. I don't how you'll get her to talk without her knowing that I've told you everything, but perhaps, on this occasion, God will forgive me for breaking confidence since I believe her future life depends on it.'

John opened the door of the carriage to let the ladies out. He was startled when he heard Mary's voice from behind.

'Hello John. Where did you find these two ladies?'

'Out visiting, Mary.' he laughed. 'I thought they looked a bit tired, so I gave them a lift home.'

Mary stood for a minute watching him and then smiled, before turning to Rose.

'This is the angel who helped me to believe that there is God again, ma. He's a very special person.'

'Stop now, Mary,' replied John, laughing. 'You might cause me to become conceited.'

'To match your big heart, John,' Mary said, warmly. 'Take care on your journey home.'

'I will, Mary, I will, but you take care now too, and remember what I told you...' he whispered in her ear ... Remember I said that the only way to find peace again will be to tell your story to those you can trust.' Mary looked away, her cheeks suddenly flushed. John got back into the carriage and drove off.

Chapter 26

Christina's uncle, Henry, was the first to arrive at the house. He had taken over the funeral arrangements, as Thomas was incapable doing anything. He was so overcome with grief.

Henry was a lot kinder in his approach with Thomas than he had been on the previous visit. 'I'm so desperately sorry, Thomas,' were his first words, as he came into the drawing room, shaking Thomas with both hands. 'I just can't imagine how you feel. What a tragedy! Beyond words.'

'Thank you, Henry. I just don't know how this could have happened to the most wonderful person in the world.'

'Have you heard from the doctor regarding what actually happened,' Henry asked, pouring himself a drink.

'We have to wait for the official post-mortem results to come through, but the doctor thinks that the baby may have been already dead for some days, or even weeks. Sadly, because she ignored the pains, she died from toxic shock - or something like that. Nobody knows for sure what happened.'

Henry put his arm around Thomas. 'We'll get through this, son. You've nothing to worry about. I'll take care of everything for you.'

'She knew that she was dying, Henry. She tried to tell me, but I wouldn't listen.' Thomas began to cry. 'I wish I had let her talk.'

'It was not for you to know, son. Death has a mind of its own and we just can't understand it sometimes. However, the important thing is that you were there for her at the end,' Henry replied softly.

Thomas just stood silently looking at the floor. Richard came into the room.

'There's someone at the door, sir. I believe it may be the undertaker,' he said quietly to Henry.

The next few days were a blur to Thomas as he had to shake hands with endless people he didn't know and pretend to be brave. Richard was always at his side, and managed the sad occasion perfectly.

The funeral was one of the biggest ever seen in the West Country with over a thousand mourners attending. She was buried beside her father in his freshly dug grave. Henry stayed for a few days after the funeral and then returned to his home to Bristol. He told Thomas that they must discuss the estate, whenever he felt up to it.

Thomas lay in bed every day till lunchtime, and was starting to drink heavily in the evenings. He and Richard often sat silently by the roaring log fire in the huge living room.

'I don't know what to do Richard,' said Thomas glumly, one evening, as he sipped his whiskey. 'I feel like I've nothing left to live for. Christina was my life.'

'Which answer do you want?' replied Richard, looking sternly at him. 'Will you allow me to speak frankly?'

'Please continue,' Thomas said, a bit startled.

Richard ventured, "Listen, my friend. This is indeed the worst possible thing that could happen to you, but it's not the end of your life. At the age of twenty-five this is only the start of new chapter. You have just become one of the wealthiest men in England - you, a country boy from rural Ireland! With that amount of wealth, you could do so much. Also, you are young enough to marry again. Do not give up hope, Thomas.'

Thomas was silent and looked at Richard in disbelief. 'I always thought the English had no heart. Now I'm sure of it.'

'You are my best and, at present, my only friend, so I have no choice but to tell you the truth - because I'm afraid you shall destroy yourself with that strong drink,' he said reprovingly.

Thomas looked long and hard at Richard, not knowing whether or not he was serious, and then burst into uncontrollable laughter. He tried, in his drunken state, to recite some old Irish poems about finding life in the quiet country, but he got all the words and lines muddled up.

'Ah. What a load of nonsense. All I need is to get away home to the sea.'

'Hmm, speaking about home, Thomas, I was thinking that, as Christmas is approaching, I might go home this year to visit my family.' There was more silence. 'I also thought that you might like to join me, and get away from here for a while.'

Sir William and Maud were entertaining some close friends from Londonderry with a full traditional meal. 'I hear you've been helping the locals, William. You're the talk of the city this past while,' said the man opposite.

'Don't you not find that a frightful drain on your resources?' Sir John's wife asked.

'Life every day is a drain on our resources, Lady Helen. I don't know why we should not share that with our local friends.'

'Friends, William?' Sir John nearly choked. 'Didn't some of your friends attempt to burn you out last year?'

'That incident came about because of my own stupidity, John, not because the locals were trying to get rid of us.'

'It certainly appeared that way to everyone else,' Helen interjected. 'I dare say most Irish people at present would like to escape from the poor governmental decisions of London which are causing the death of hundreds of thousands of Irish people. Irritatingly, they see us as part of the English problem. They hate us.'

'I think if we were to take you to visit the forty-five families which are living on our estate, Helen, you might find a very different way of looking at things,' Maud said, sternly.

'Well, we don't seem to be as bad here in the north as the west and south of the country.'

Sir John tried to ease the tension that was gathering between the diners. 'It is quite appalling that grain, which is sitting in large quantities in England, cannot be shipped across immediately.'

'There's more to this potato blight than meets the eye,' Sir William responded, 'but perhaps, since we are enjoying such a fine banquet, this is not the best time to think about what's going on here right now.'

'The government seems determined to collect the revenue due to them from estates like yours, William,' Sir John said, ignoring his attempt at distraction. 'It's going to make life very difficult for a lot of people like us who are relying on rent from out tenants.'

'I wonder if they're doing the same in Wales and Scotland,' replied Sir William, getting cross. 'They seem to treat Ireland as a poor relation.'

'How long will you be able to hold on, William?' asked Lady Helen.

'I don't know for sure. Three months perhaps. No one can tell.' The butlers came and cleared the table and began to serve the main course. Sir William was glad to be able to change the conversation.

Rose went out to the front yard to see where Mary was as it was time for dinner. She found her putting the last of the turf that was stacked by the side of the cottage into the open dry shed. It was bitterly cold and, with winter approaching, it was vital that the turf was kept dry. Mary was working like a machine and looked exhausted. Rose came up behind her and grabbed her arms from behind.

'It's dinner time, Mary. That's enough for today.'

Mary turned to look at her mother with great sadness in her eyes. She wiped her brow and threw the last few pieces of turf onto the top of the pile.

'I'll come now, Ma. That should see us through the rest of the winter.'

'God will see us through the rest of the winter, Mary. It's time for you to rest now.'

'I can't rest, Ma. I must do this,' she replied. God expects this off me. I failed Him badly

'That isn't the God that I taught you about, Mary. He expects nothing from us but our friendship and love. There isn't anything that we can do to add to what He has already done for us.'

'I can never forget, Ma. I have dreams about it every night.'

'Then tell me what happened Mary.'

'I can't, Ma. You might never want to know me again,' Mary said, as tears welled up in her eyes.

Rose took Mary's arms forcefully in hers and looked straight into her eyes. 'Right. It's time now Mary, I'm not going to see you destroy your life by letting the past hold you in prison when I know very well it wasn't your fault.'

'What do you mean? What are you talking about?' Mary answered, sharply.

'Because … ' Rose paused and softened her tone '… Because I know what happened to you.'

Mary pulled away from her mother and was angry. 'I suppose John told you - after he promised me he would never tell anyone!'

'We forced him to tell us Mary. We were worried sick about you. But he didn't tell us everything. We want you to tell us everything now, Mary,' Rose said firmly. 'It's time for you to live again, Mary, and to live you must. You must confront the past, and then let it go.' They walked into the cottage where Bridget had dinner waiting for them. Martha came and put her arm around her sister, placing her head on her shoulder.

'We must think about Christmas, everyone,' Bridget announced, sensing it was time to lighten the conversation. 'It'll be on us in a few days and we need to gather extra food in as we might have to feed some of our neighbours.' They all sat at the table quietly. Mary knew that the time had now come to share about what happened to her in New York, but she was dreading it greatly.

When they finished talking, Rose held her daughter tightly. There were tears in the eyes of all present and, in the early hours of the morning, they all sat huddled together, hugging. 'Mary, you will never have to suffer such pain again, my precious girl,' cried Rose, as she stroked her daughter's hair. 'Listen to me, my darling, none of this is your fault. None of it, Mary, and God has rescued your life for a great purpose.'

'Yes,' she nodded, quietly. 'Maybe you're right.'

Rose continued, 'Jesus came to earth and showed his great love for us by giving his life for us, Mary, and while it was a terrible thing, there was a greater purpose.' She paused and stared at the dying embers of the fire. 'Some day you will understand, my sweet girl, but now you may even be able to use this terrible experience to try and help others who may have the same kind of bad things happen to them.'

'Are you absolutely sure that God still loves me, Ma?' Mary sobbed.

'Oh, he does, Mary. So much so that he sent John to find you and rescue you.' They hugged and then went to bed. Suddenly Mary felt a deep peace come over her and strong arms wrapped tightly around her as she drifted off into a deep sleep. She knew now that she was never alone.

Chapter 27

April 1847

It was a warm Spring day, and Thomas was out with his gardener explaining new plans he had drawn up to extend Christina's rather lavish fountains. Richard pulled up in the carriage and joined them.

'How's the dam proceeding, Richard?' Thomas enquired.

'Nearly finished, Thomas' Richard said, triumphantly. 'It's a magnificent piece of work, I have to say". They followed my design and used the natural neck of the valley, which means the construction work was very easy. They'll now leave it to settle for a few months and then start to fill the lake, which should be well up by Christmas this year.'

'Are you sure it'll be strong enough, Richard? That dam will have tremendous pressure on it, you know.'

'They had over a thousand workers on it and machinery I never knew existed!' Richard said, sitting down on edge of the fountain. Thomas turned to the gardener and continued with his instructions. When he had finished he and Richard walked back to the house.

'It's lunchtime, Richard, and you and I need to talk,' Thomas said, solemnly.

'You're talking to me right now,' replied Richard, in his usual teasing manner.

'I have a plan,' Thomas said, entering the front door and ordering lunch from the butler.

'I'm going home, Richard,' Thomas said softly.

Richard was quiet. He looked at him, both surprised and concerned.

Thomas waited for a response, but nothing came. 'Do you understand, Richard? I'm going home,' he repeated, decisively.

'Yes, I heard you. You're going home, you said, but you are home, Thomas, so I'm confused.'

Thomas paused and turned, looking Richard in the face. 'I need to go home to live with my people, Richard. This is not my life.' Richard now got very uneasy as he wondered what was coming next. 'This is my plan, and you can tell me what you think of it.' Thomas said trying to sound enthusiastic. Richard waited.

'I am one of the wealthiest landowners in England and, even after we pay Christina's death duties, there will be enough money and revenue to run this estate for a very long time. I had a long talk with Henry and we came to an agreement. This estate has been in his family for hundreds of years and I have no right to it, Richard.' Thomas paused and looked at his friend.

'I have handed it back to his family in return for a very large sum of money that I can live on for the rest of my life. I want to go home and buy my mother and my neighbour a big house with land for them to farm. Henry agreed, therefore, to entrust all the affairs of this estate into your very capable hands, and will pay you a lot of money in return.' Richard was shocked! He was also getting upset now as well as he neither wanted to lose his best friend or to have this responsibility.

'I couldn't do that, Thomas,' he choked. 'I'm twenty-four and come from working class folks, as you've seen. I could never suddenly pretend to be titled!'

'You are not going to get a title'. Thomas laughed. 'Just run the place for Henry and send me a big cheque every year. I'm sure you will find a nice country lass who will gladly come and look after you, and every few years I'll come back to make sure you haven't flooded the countryside,' Thomas joked, patting him on the back. 'Either that, or I'll ask him to advertise the post and give you a job as head gardener.'

Richard turned to look at him 'I couldn't do this without you, Thomas. You've been so good to me since we started with the ordnance survey company. You have always been there to give me advice. We're a team. I couldn't do this without you. You're my only friend.' Richards eyes were growing red.

'I'll still be here, Richard, in spirit, and then now again in person as well, whenever I feel the urge to share a beer with an English gentleman."

'You're serious, Thomas, aren't you? I can see it in your eyes.' Richard said, sadly

'Yes, my dear friend. I'm serious. I'd like to leave next week.'

Richard went very quiet and turned and stared out the window. 'What would I do, living all alone here, with such a huge house and six thousand acres?' Richard said, panic beginning to rise in his voice.

'Go into town next week and look for the most beautiful girl in town. If necessary, you could even pay her to marry you,' Thomas said lightly.

'Is that what you think of me?' laughed Richard.

'Once word gets about that there's a twenty-four year old bachelor living alone in this mansion, you'll have a trail of women asking for jobs here that don't even exist so, before they do, go and chose your bride.'

'It's not that easy, my friend. I don't want a wife yet. I feel like I'm part of your family.' Thomas knew that he was leaving his best friend and just realised that this might not be the best time to tease.

'Maybe you could come to Ireland for a few months.'

'That sounds more like it, Thomas, only I might find an Irish lass and not want to come home.' replied Richard smiling. They hugged each other before going into the dining room for lunch.

Richard had the finest coach waiting at the door the following week, and the butler had Thomas's bags packed on the back. He came out the door and went straight to the coach. 'I haven't told any of the staff that I'm going away, Richard, as I think it's better that they don't know,' Thomas said, facing Richard, who now had tears in his eyes. 'When I'm settled in my new house you must come and visit Ireland, Richard. Despite the potato blight that is destroying the country, Donegal is still an enchanting place'

'I shall miss you greatly, Thomas,' Richard replied, choking on his words. 'I have never had such a good friend, and will likely never find one again. God be with you.' They hugged, and Thomas got into the coach, before ordering the driver to leave immediately. Richard stood staring as the coach disappeared slowly down the driveway.

Sir William sat in the breakfast room with his head down. Maud came into the room and sat down opposite him and proceeded to butter some toast. 'You look glum William. What's the matter?

William looked at her then spoke slowly and sadly. 'We're ruined Maud.' He paused to finish his coffee. 'I have just received a letter from the government: If we cannot pay the land tax, our estate has been forfeited and is going to be handed back to the Crown.' Maud sat silently, slowly sipping her tea. 'What does that mean in practical terms, William?'

'It means, Maud, that our money has run out. We thought this might happen one day, this time it really has. We are requested to be out of the property entirely within a week or the Crown bailiffs will escort us out. We're ruined, finished, homeless, whatever you want to call it, Maud. It's over.' Maud got up and put her arms around Sir William's shoulders.

'We shall go to my family's old estate in England, William. We have no other choice.' William just sat with his head in his hands.

'I shall have to go and explain to our new tenants that they will all have to leave. It isn't just we who will be homeless. At least we have somewhere to go. They have nothing!'

'It just doesn't seem right, during one of the country's worst disasters where hundreds of thousands of people are dying, that the English government should act like this.' Maud said. 'Can't we contact people in London?'

'It would appear that, with so many people dying, many landlords now receive no rent and are in danger of going the same way.'

'I wager that not one English politician has ever set foot in Ireland since the potato blight began. If this disaster had happened over there, things would be very different.'

William got up from the table. 'I shall go and talk to my friends personally.' He called John and they both set off to the houses at different parts of the estate while Maud ordered boxes to begin the long process of packing their valuables.

Chapter 28

Thomas stood on the deck on the port side of the ship as it made its way up the river Liffey, into the heart of Dublin. Despite being tremendously sad to leave his friend, Richard, in England, he was elated when he took a deep breath of the Irish air as the ship pulled into its berth in the harbour. The first thing that struck him was how busy the port was with so many ships unloading goods and passengers. There didn't appear to be any sign of the great potato blight which he had heard was affecting Dublin city so badly.

As the harbour men tied up the ship, he could smell the river Liffey, and the water looked almost black. He could see smoke coming from nearly every house in the city, causing a fog to hang over many of the streets. He found himself dreaming as he looked out at the hills on the west side of the city. but just then a steward called to him and told him the ship was disembarking the passengers.

After he walked off the gangway he called a taxi and asked him to take him to the land valuation office. As they drove along the streets away from the harbour he could see groups of people begging in the streets – something never seen in Ireland before. He asked the taxi driver what had befallen these folks and was told that they were starving people who had come in from the country down south because there was no food in most towns outside the cities.

The land valuation office was in a very old governmental building which was badly run down. Thomas asked the taxi driver to wait as he climbed the steps to go in through a large green door. The corridor was lit by only one sky light window and weaved its way down steps to several large drab rooms. He entered the first room and a man in a worn tweed suit was sitting at a desk piled high with papers. He was busy filling his pipe with tobacco. Another man was at the back of the room was trying to find a file from a long shelf of dusty documents. Thomas went and stood in front of the man and announced:

'Good day, sir. I would like to buy some land in Donegal.'

The man didn't answer but, puffing on his pipe, he began searching through a large pile of sheets in front of him. Thomas waited a good minute before repeating his statement, to which the man replied, 'I heard you.' Then silence again for another minute.

Eventually he looked up and asked, 'What sort of land in Donegal?'

'A large amount of land to farm and upon which I can build a house.'

The man looked at Thomas and then continued searching through his papers. 'How would you pay for this land?' the man asked, barely disguising the fact that he saw Thomas as a waste of his precious time.

Thomas was now getting a little irritated, and raised his voice slightly. 'With money, obviously.' He looked up, puffing his pipe.

'There are very few people buying land anywhere right now. You might have noticed, the country is on its knees, and you come in and tell me you want to buy a lot of land in Donegal?'

Thomas was now annoyed at not being believed. 'Yes, I want a sizable amount of land in Donegal. I already own six thousand acres in England.' The man nearly choked on his pipe and suddenly got nervous.

'Pardon me, sir, but what part of Donegal would you be thinking about?'

'Maybe I could show you on a map.' He rose and told Thomas to follow him to the right side of the room where there was a large newly drawn map of Ireland hanging on the wall.

'This map has recently been sent to us by the ordnance survey company in England, so it's fully up to date,' he announced proudly.

'I know,' replied Thomas. 'I was one of the surveyors on the team that made it.' The man looked at him sideways, and continued puffing on his pipe.

'There are four different areas of Donegal, so once you tell me which part of the county we can then pull out the map for that place.' Thomas pointed to Inishowen which was north of Londonderry. The man went away out the back and returned five minutes later with a new map of Inishowen.

'Why has this area on the east side got a red circle around it?' Thomas enquired, curiously.

'It used to belong to an English landlord who didn't pay his taxes to the Crown. He is now ruined, and they've taken the land and his house from him.'

'Who would that English landlord be?' asked Thomas

'I cannot give information like that to you, sir. It's confidential.'

'Is it for sale?' Thomas asked, apprehensively.

'It can be purchased from the Crown, but the price will have to include the money that is owed from the previous owner.'

'How much would that be?' Thomas asked, impatiently.

'I'll have to dig out the files. It might take me some time.'

'I have all the time in the world - if it's the property I think it may be.' Thomas' heart was now pounding. The man seemed annoyed at having to go for the files so called his assistant from the back.

'Michael, get me the files belonging to the foreclosure of the estate in Inishowen.

The other man grunted and disappeared. 'You may have a long wait,' the man said, gruffly.

It was nearly an hour before the man appeared carrying a box of files and dumped them down on the front desk. 'These are Sir William Campbell's files' he said. Thomas' heart missed a beat. So, he was correct!

'The owner moves out of the property next week and we have been instructed to sell the property for ten thousand pounds, which includes all the money owed by the landlord.'

'That's a huge sum of money for an estate that loses money every year and is in an area of non-commercial value.'

'That's the price, take it or leave it,' he said, turning back to his desk.

'I'll take it,' Thomas said immediately.

'How will you pay for it?' he asked, half expecting Thomas to leave quickly.

'I shall write you a cheque now for it, provided I don't need a legal person to deal with it.'

'I am a legal person,' the man answered tersely. 'Are you certain that you can afford that - at your age?' Thomas was getting cross and threw the cheque book down in front of him.

'Never judge a book by its cover, sir. I could pay ten times this amount and it wouldn't make a difference to my wealth,' he blurted out. 'Now sign the papers, please.' Thomas wrote out the cheque, while the man grumbled to himself and disappeared out the back again. When he returned he shoved the envelope in front of Thomas.

'These are the deeds to the estate. They will not become legal until your cheque has been lodged and accepted by the Crown bank.'

Thomas lifted the envelope and left. The taxi was still waiting for him and the driver was asleep in the back. He was taken to a hotel in the centre of Dublin where he had dinner, and then turned in for an early night. He would sleep peacefully tonight. He would now, at last, allow his mind to recall the day Sir William's men put him and his mother out of their home and burnt the roof. He had his revenge now, and it felt sweet. He smiled to himself as he imagined how much he would enjoy telling the English landlord, who was about to be evicted, that he was the new owner of his estate. His evil landlord would now be homeless, just as his family were five years before – and he would be living in his home! Thomas slept soundly that night.

Chapter 29

Mary was helping her mother, Rose, hang washing on the line. The day was cold, but dry. They were discussing whether they should plough the field at the side of the house for a potato crop.

'What would happen if the blight comes again like last year?' Mary asked anxiously.

'I don't know Mary, but sure what have we got to lose? The seed will not keep till next year and we now have enough other produce to live on if it fails again.'

'I hear the potato blight's very bad down the west, Ma. Donegal has not been the worst hit.' Bridget and Mary came out of the front door and beat some old mats against the wall to knock the dirt off them. Mary was about to say something when they heard a horse and trap coming up the lane.

'Now who's that at this time of the day? Sure ...' Bridget started, but was cut short by who she saw. Thomas drove the trap right into the yard. She stood transfixed. 'Do you not recognise your own son, Ma?' he called. Bridget ran towards him, arms outstretched. He looked surprised to see Mary.

'Thomas! Thomas! Is that really you?' She threw her arms around him, weeping loudly.

Mary stood silently, in shock, but then slipped quietly inside the house again, her heart racing. Rose ran to hug Thomas.

When all the hugging was over, Thomas turned to Rose and asked, 'Why did Mary run into the house?' Rose took Thomas by the arm as they walked towards the front door.

'Give her time Thomas. She's been to hell and back in America and it took her a long time to talk to us. She's been very badly affected by what happened to her there.'

'Why? What happened to her, Rose? You must tell me!' Thomas said, anxiously.

'She'll tell you herself one day, Thomas, but you mustn't force her. For now, she may not even speak to you, so please try and understand. It isn't you.'

Thomas looked very concerned and stared at the floor for a long time. 'I should never have gone away, Rose. I've gained the whole world but lost everything.'

'Never say that, Thomas,' replied Rose, thoughtfully. 'You're only coming twenty-five and you've got your whole life ahead of you. If you use the experiences that you've been through for your good, then God will help you have a great future.'

'If you had been through what I have, Rose, you might not believe in your God anymore. For me, I'm just numb, and I feel completely lost right now.'

Bridget was listening to the conversation and put her arm around his shoulder. 'We are now all together again, son, and God has spared us for a purpose, while many people around us have died.'

'I wish I had your faith,' he said sadly, and slumped down in the soft chair in the corner. 'It's so good to be home.'

'I'll make something to eat, son,' said Bridget, going to the kitchen table. 'If I had known you were coming home we could have had a feast. Maybe after dinner you can tell us all about your adventure.'

'You would never believe it, Ma. It's been like a dream.'

Rose went along the corridor to Mary's room where she found her crying on her bed. She sat down on the bed beside her and stroked her head. 'It's all right, darling,' she said softly. 'I know it's hard, but time will heal your pain.'

'It's not that. It's seeing Thomas brought everything back to me.'

'Why would seeing Thomas do that, Mary?'

'Because I loved him so much, Ma, but now everything's changed,' she sobbed. 'He should never have left.'

'He took an opportunity that any young man would have taken, and he has done well, but he's home now, Mary. Hopefully this is where he will now stay.'

'He's home now, Ma, but he left me to ruin my life in America,' Mary answered, anger in her voice.

'You went away to provide money for us, Mary, and it was never your fault that you were kidnapped and treated so badly.'

'I should never have been so nice to the man on the ship. He probably thought I liked him,' Mary mused.

'You must stop thinking like that, Mary. That man was only nice to you so that he could use you for his own evil gain when you got to New York.'

'I can never look at a man again.'

'The only way out of your prison, Mary, is to ask God to help you forgive the men who used you,' Rose said, standing up.

'How can I forgive when my life is ruined? I will never forget those evil men!' Mary said sharply

'I didn't say forget, Mary, for you never will forget, but if you forgive it will release you,' Rose said, moving to the door.

'I still love Thomas, Ma, but I just shudder at the thought of any man touching me.'

'If Thomas is the man that God has for you, Mary, then he will help you, and one day you will feel like a new person. For now, at least, be civil to him, for I know that he has had sadness in his life too.'

Rose left her and walked back to the kitchen where dinner was ready. They all sat down at the table and, after Rose said a blessing, they began to eat. To everyone surprise, five minutes later Mary came and sat at the end of the table, but she didn't once look at Thomas for the entire meal.

Sir William and Maud were in their dining room finishing their dinner when John came in. 'My lord, everything is ready for the morning, and I thought I would take my leave of you tonight as I do not wish to see you go in the morning.' Sir William stood up with tears in his eyes and shook John's hand.

'I've never had a more faithful friend and worker than you, John. I shall miss you the most. I have written a reference for you, and I hope you find work soon.'

'Thank you, sir' replied John, staring at the floor. 'This home has been my life, and you have been like parents to me. I will never forget you either, and I want you to know that the whole community believes that you both are among some of the finest people who ever lived in Donegal. The wishes of everyone here are that you will both be happy in your new life back in England. With that, John left the room and William turned to Maud:

'I don't believe this is happening, Maud. Perhaps we will wake up in the morning and find it has all been just a bad dream.'

When Mary finished eating she said goodnight and went back to her room. Rose told Martha to get changed and go to bed, after she cleared the dinner dishes. Thomas stretched and said he was tired, but Bridget made him sit by the fire. 'Now' she began. 'You're not going to saunter in here after five years and then go to bed without telling us your story, so you'd better start - and I mean all of it.' Thomas was taken aback, but knew he couldn't argue with his mother.

Rose and Bridget sat transfixed as he told of all his experiences over the past five years. Two hours later, they were still talking, asking questions and crying.

'I must go to bed now.' Thomas stood up. 'I have one important thing to do in the morning.'

'What's that?' asked Bridget, curiously.

'I'm going over the hill to watch Sir William evicted from the estate - which I now own - and remind him of what he did to us five years ago.' he announced, triumphantly.

'What on earth are you talking about, Thomas? Why did you say, "the estate I own"? You don't own any estate, Thomas!' Bridget looked at him, concerned. Had he lost his mind?

'I bought his entire estate, Ma. I heard that the Crown is about to evict him, and I want to go and witness his departure. Perhaps this will remind him of what he did to us.' Ignoring the first part of his announcement regarding buying an estate, putting it down to some strange fantasy he had had regarding his desire for revenge, Bridget was more concerned with what he was planning to do.

'You'll do no such thing, Thomas Sweeney!' she shouted angrily. Thomas was taken aback by this reaction.

'He deserves it! Have you forgotten what it felt like to watch our home burn? He did this to us!' Rose knew there was going to be an argument, so she stood in front of Thomas.

'Thomas' she began, 'you have every right to do that tomorrow. It was a very cruel thing that Sir William did, but let me tell you this, and then you can decide what you want to do. Sir William didn't authorise his bailiff to destroy your home, and he was enraged when he found out about it. He came here to apologise and offer your mother a new home, but she decided she would stay here as we had lost both our husbands and we needed each other for company.

'When the crops failed last year, Sir William took in forty-five families - over two hundred people, in fact - and put them in houses and sheds on his estate. When the houses were full he kept some of them in his own house. Not only did he house them, but he and Maud cooked meals for them and gave them jobs, so they didn't feel like they were beggars.

They are now held in the highest esteem in Donegal, and even some of the other landlords began to imitate them. Because they refused to collect rents they are now bankrupt and are being forced by the government to move to England to live in a tiny house. As a matter of fact, it's near to where you lived.' Rose paused, as she noticed the change in Thomas's expression.

'If you go tomorrow and gloat at their loss, then both Bridget and I would be very angry because, not only did Sir William do all this, but he paid his estate manager, John, to go to New York for two months to find and rescue Mary. We would never have seen her again if he had not found her.' Thomas sat up at this mention of Mary.

'You keep saying this about Mary. Why on earth did she need rescued?' Thomas asked. impatiently.

'She will tell you one day, Thomas, but until then you must know that her situation was much graver than your own. You must know, also, that she owes her life to Sir William.'

'I want to know the truth, since it was probably because my leaving that all this, whatever it was, happened.' Thomas was troubled, but knew he would have to wait until the time was right to hear what that was.

Chapter 30

Rose was up at dawn, and was about to put the kettle on the fire when she heard the horse and trap going down the lane. She ran to the door, and was in time to see Thomas turn the corner and head towards Moville. Bridget appeared behind her, and the two of them held each other's arms. They knew Thomas was away to watch the eviction of Sir William, and they were so ashamed.

Thomas pushed the horse hard on the mountain track and cracked the whip a few times. He was angry. He was angry with himself for coming home, he was angry with Mary, who wouldn't even speak to him, he was angry at Sir William who ruined his life and he was angry with God who took away his father and best friend. He galloped the horse down the last part of the track to Greencastle until the horse was exhausted and beginning to stumble. Eventually he allowed it to rest for a few minutes.

He could see the sun rising over Lough Foyle to his left and a small sailing ship was passing Moville harbour on its way to Londonderry. Thomas had intended to vent his furious anger at Sir William but now, as he stared out across Moville Bay, he reflected on those good people who were so kind to him in England. Suddenly, he was more upset than angry.

He turned into the long driveway of Sir William's estate and was surprised to see the spring flowers beginning to come out early and the rhododendrons blooming. As he approached the house he could see Sir William's grand coach waiting at the front door, with two other coaches loaded with suit cases and boxes all ready to go.

He pulled his trap up and blocked the exit of the coach. Then he alighted. As he approached the front door, Sir William and Maud came out the door saying goodbye to their last few remaining staff. Thomas deliberately stood in front of the coach with his arms folded. As the couple approached him he shouted, 'Do you know who I am?'

'No' replied Sir William, surprised at this intrusion.

'I am Thomas Sweeney from Kinnego Bay.' He paused, and then dropped his arms. 'You put my mother and me out of our home five years ago and then burnt the roof. You left us homeless and destitute!' William now looked alarmed, and wondered if this young man might be armed.

'I am really sorry about that, Mr. Sweeney. It happened without my consent, although I don't expect you to believe that. I know that you've got every right to be angry.'

'Do you recall that I told your bailiff, as he burned my home, that one day I would have my revenge - that I would, one day, watch you being evicted? I vowed that one day you would get a taste of what it's like to lose your home.'

'Well, as you see, we're leaving now, so you have your revenge,' Sir William replied sadly, and continued to walk to the coach.

'You don't understand. The Crown has evicted you, certainly, but what you don't know is that I now own your estate. I will live here now instead of you. This is my revenge.' Sir William and Maud stopped and looked at Thomas in disbelief. 'I bought this estate last week in Dublin.'

'Don't be ridiculous, son. Where would get that sort of money?' Sir William shook his head.

'I have the deeds to this estate,' Thomas said, producing a large brown envelope. He went over to the carriage and handed them to Sir William.

'Where did you get these legal documents, Mr. Sweeney?' Sir William glanced over the document.

'I told you, Sir William. I bought this property last week in Dublin.' Thomas walked up to William and looked him in the face.

'Well' Sir William repeated, sadly. 'It seems that you really do have your revenge, son. I don't know how this is possible, but hope it will make up for what I did to you in the past.' He looked sadly back at his house, handing the deeds back to Thomas – but, to their surprise, he shook his head, backing away.

'I don't want them.' he said. 'I am giving you your home back, sir.'

William and Maud looked at Thomas. They wondered if he was playing a cruel trick on them. 'Please, son, we need to go now. This is very hard for us, and we would rather you let us drive on.' William tried to move, but Thomas moved in front of him.

'I am giving you back your home Sir William, take the deeds.' Thomas pushed the envelope back into his hands. 'I believe you've rescued my best friend, Mary, from New York and that you've cared for my dying neighbours.' Thomas said thankfully. 'I want you to move away from this coach and return to your new home.'

'This is a very cruel joke,' William said gruffly. 'Please we must go now.'

'Sir William. Please allow me to explain. I came into a fortune in your country, that I didn't really deserve, and now I want to thank you for what you've done,' Thomas said, moving to the door and holding a hand out for Maud to step down from the coach.

'I am serious, Sir William. The house is yours' Thomas said, now smiling.

Sir William took Maud's hand and led her out of the coach. He stood in front of Thomas. They were speechless.

'I would like you to stay in your home - but with one condition' Thomas ventured. 'That is provided I can have thirty acres at Greencastle to build my own house overlooking the sea. I also insist that you allow me to give you advice on the running of the estate to make it profitable again as I have done with the estate I once owned in England. I'll invest a lot of money to help you over the next two years to make it great again, as if it were my own, but the estate will always belong to you. The next time I'm in Dublin I'll make it legal at the land office. Oh, and, by the way, I have also paid off the debt to the Crown.' Sir William and Maud were speechless!

'Why are you doing this, Thomas?' asked Maud, wiping away tears.

'Because I now can, ma'am,' Thomas replied, dropping his gaze to the ground, 'and because, in my short life, I have met many of your people from over the water who were immensely kind to me. It's also because I am entirely grateful for what you have done for my people.'

'It would cost thousands of pounds to make this estate viable again,' Sir William said. 'It may not be possible.'

'I know Sir William,' replied Thomas, 'but I think we could both have fun spending that amount, don't you?' he laughed. 'Now get your staff to take your bags in again and let's get you out of this rain.'

William and Maud moved to shake Thomas's hand but he had already returned to his trap. 'I expect to be invited to your first house party when you get things sorted' he shouted cheerily, climbing up into the trap. 'I will send you money in the next few days.'

Sir William and Maud stood silently in the rain as they watched Thomas disappear down the driveway. 'Welcome home, sir,' said the maid, who had overheard the whole conversation.

The sun shone brightly as Thomas travelled home over the hill. Suddenly he felt like a huge weight had lifted off his shoulders. He looked up at the sky and found himself singing the words of a song he had heard Rose sing many years ago, 'Amazing grace, how sweet the sound, that saved a wretch like me!' What had just happened back there? Something stirred within him and he felt a deep peace he had never felt before. A deep awareness swept over him that he was finally home.

The rain stopped and the sky had turned blue by the time Thomas got back over the mountain. He stopped the trap in the yard and unhitched the exhausted horse. His mother came out the front door and stood staring at him.

'What?' Thomas asked.

'How could you be so mean to a man who has done so much for us?' Bridget started, shaking with anger.

Thomas didn't answer, but let her continue. 'It's enough for the poor man to lose his house, but for you to go and be a witness to his tragedy was a cruel thing to do!' Thomas came close to her, looking her in the eye.

'I gave him back his estate, Ma. Now what are ye scolding about?'

'You did what?' Bridget exclaimed.

'I have a lot of money, Ma. I own the whole estate, so I gave it back to them and told them they could live there forever.'

'Oh, my son!' Bridget started to cry. 'I just knew my real son would come home. I'm so, so proud of you!'

Rose appeared, and Bridget told her what Thomas had done. 'You did the right thing, Thomas. God will bless you for what you've done today.'

'God has already blessed me, Rose, by bringing me home to where I belong. I know that now,' replied Thomas firmly as he took the horse and brought it around to the field at the side of the house, releasing it. He came back to the front of the house where Rose was helping Martha feed the chickens. 'Where's Mary?' he asked Rose.

'She went down to the bay. It's the only place she seems happy these days.' He turned and started to walk down the lane.

'Leave her alone, son,' called Bridget after him 'She isn't ready to talk yet.' Thomas didn't look round but just kept walking. When he got to the top of the field he could see Mary sitting in the place they used to sit together. Suddenly his heart broke, and tears appeared on his cheeks. He stood for a long time watching her, before he walked quietly through the grass until he could almost touch her long, shiny, black hair.

Mary glanced round nervously but made no move to run away. Thomas sat down very close beside her and picked a long piece of grass, putting it in his mouth. He touched her hand as they sat looking out at the blue ocean with the waves breaking on Kinnego Strand down below.

'I have something for you, Mary,' Thomas said quietly.

Mary glanced shyly at him as he handed her the St. Bridget's cross which she had given him when he left for England. She sat staring at the cross for about a minute. Then she took it gently from him and kissed it, tears in her eyes.

'Where did you go Thomas?' Mary asked, her voice full of emotion. 'Why did you not come home to me?'

Thomas looked out to sea, 'I don't know Mary. My life away seemed like a dream - a very long dream. In these five years I feel like I've lived an entire lifetime,' he said, sadly. They sat gazing at the ocean for a long time. Then Thomas asked softly, 'Mary, can you ever forgive me?' Mary's bottom lip began to quiver.

'I'll try, Thomas, but it is you who must forgive me. I've lived a life that is far from all I was brought up to believe in, and I'm broken inside'.

'It's been a long road home Mary, but we're home now'. Thomas smiled 'This is where I belong, and this is where we can begin again.' Mary responded by resting her head on his shoulder as they sat quietly together staring out to sea.

Printed in Great Britain
by Amazon

Thomas dreams of a new and more exciting life far from his Donegal homestead. After tragedy strikes his wishes are fulfilled, and he gains all he ever wants - but at what price? He's catapulted into a world completely foreign to him, but he's now trapped; and what of his childhood friend, Mary? Little does he know she's in grave danger in America; her family struggling through the potato famine back home. He must return and avenge the English landlord who treated his family so cruelly, but how can this ever be possible now?

ISBN 9781973549420

90000

9 781973 549420